Lori's Memories

Drake Wines, Volume 2.5

Chelle pimblott

Published by Chelle pimblott, 2021.

LORI'S MEMORIES

First edition. June 30, 2021.

Written by Chelle pimblott.

To my book bitches, without you, I wouldn't be writing!

To my editor in chief, thank you for all that you do and it goes way beyond being a sounding board and the editing.

To my family, thanks for letting me forget to feed you every now and then!!

I'd also like to dedicate this book to those we have lost to Cancer:

Kirsty, Yvonne, Evelyn, Annie and the many more that we've all lost way too soon xxxxx

PLEASE NOTE

LORI'S MEMORIES

was written by an Australian author, in Australia English.

As such you may assume there are some spelling errors within, however it's just how we spell things downunder.

*****

Part .1.

Lori

Dear Savannah,

By the time you read this, well you'll officially be a Drake and you'll already know how my story ends, but I wanted to tell you the rest of the story. I want you to understand why I did the things I did and how we ended up where we did.

From the moment I found out I was pregnant with you, my first and only child, things didn't go as I'd planned. Not that I'm complaining, not for a second! You were my biggest blessing and I wouldn't have changed a thing, it's just as the old saying goes, 'life is what happens while you're making plans'. That kind of sums up my life.

By now, you know that Logan Drake is your father. In fact, I never hid the fact that was your Dad's name but you've lived most of your life with him now and his husband, Jules. I have no doubt that they've given you everything life has to offer, including the unconditional love of two of the best men I know.

It starts in our last year at university and ends with me asking Logan the biggest favour any person could ask of another. Especially when they didn't know they had a daughter for the first seven years of her life. I want you to know that was *my* decision. I don't know if Logan has talked to you about how or *when* he found out he was a father but I want you to know that the minute he knew you existed, he wanted to know you. I have no doubt that if he's told you anything, he's always painted *me* in the best light that he could. That's just the kind of man your father is and while I didn't get long to get to know his husband, I know he wouldn't be with someone who wasn't a good man.

I hope that he gave you this collection of letters when he thought you were ready to read them. Who I am kidding? I know he did!

I want you to remember that I love you, always and forever.

1

I love you to the moon and back baby girl,

Mum xx

PS: If you've read this Logan and I'm pretty sure you did before you gave it to Savannah, I want you to know that I love you. I always loved you and I want to thank you for giving me the best gift you could have given me. Savannah. Our daughter.

My last year of University

When we first met, I couldn't believe Logan was interested in *me*. There were girls all over campus that wanted to be with him, most would have given anything to have a chance with him. Rumours surrounded the guy all the girls and a lot of the guys, wanted to be. I knew of a few girls that went on dates with him but they never really went any further. He had a reputation of a bit of a ladies man, so when he asked me out, I hesitated. For some reason, we lasted six months but there was always this nagging feeling in the back of my mind that we were more like best friends than lovers.

To be honest though, I pushed all my doubts away because Logan Drake chose *me*, and he was every girl's idea of a dream guy. Honestly, he was built, confident without being arrogant, intelligent with the smarts to be cool about it, and sensitive. I should have known he was too good to be true when he was in touch with his feelings. I mean, the man cried when I broke up with him!

"Why?" He asks, as one tear slides down his cheek.

"It's just not working Logan, you can *feel* that, right?" I ask him, desperately wanting him to understand.

"I thought we had something great to be honest." He looks so freaking sad and I don't know how I'm going to make him understand without hurting him because in this moment, I realise he doesn't know himself.

"Look, we're great friends but don't you think we're missing something?"

"Missing what?"

"Ummmm chemistry?"

"So, you're saying the sex isn't great?" He asks, the look on his face morphing from sad to mortified. "I mean, it wasn't perfect but we can build on that, right?"

"No." I shake my head. "I don't think we can Logan. It's just not there and I know that if you *really* think about it, you'll know it's the truth."

"So, that's it? You're telling me that the sex sucks, therefore our relationship is over? That six months is worth nothing?" I flinch, not because he's angry but because he *isn't* angry or emotional about what I just told him. Therefore proving to me that there just isn't the passion between us that I want in a relationship.

"It's not because the sex sucks, Logan, it's because there's no connection between us beyond being friends. You understand that, right?"

"So, you're saying you want to be friends then?"

"Sure." He raises an eyebrow at me, questioning whether I truly mean to agree with him. "Yes Logan, I really want to be friends with you, but I don't think we should be together anymore. I think we both know that I'm not the right *person* for you." He closes his eyes and nods. I thought he was going to fight me a little more, but when he opens his eyes, and they connect with mine, I see that he too understood what I was trying to say. He was sad but he knew it was for the best.

"OK. I'm sorry I couldn't be what you wanted or needed Lori. I never meant to hurt you, or waste your time."

"Ohh Logan, you didn't, we had a lot of fun together."

"Just not good enough, huh?"

"That's not true, we're just not right for each other Logan. You and I weren't meant to be lovers and I'm pretty sure you know that." He didn't reply. All he did was nod and I couldn't resist giving him one last hug. Logan Drake gives great hugs and I had an overwhelming need to feel it one more time. Burying my face into the crook of his neck and closing my eyes, I enjoyed every second of his bear hug.

"I'm sorry, Lori. Know that in my own way, I love you." He says quietly, his cheek resting on the crown of my head.

"I know, Logan and I love you too." I told him as I let out a sigh as I sink into his embrace. I enjoy being held by him for another minute, then step out of it. Far enough away that neither of us can reach out and touch the other easily. I need to make this break and I need to do it now before I can convince myself that we can make this work but I think we both recognise that if the relationship goes on for any longer, it's going to end with more heartache than it is right now. "Goodbye Logan."

"Bye Lori."

I turn away from the man I just spent the last six months with and walk away from him without looking back. I'm not sure where I'm headed, I've never been on this side of campus before. What I do know is that I need to be away from Logan right now, so I just keep walking.

I see an empty bench seat in the shade of a tree, and make a beeline straight for it. I drop onto the seat and just sit there for a few minutes not really looking at or seeing anything. I know I did the right thing, I'm not the right woman for Logan.

I start laughing and I must look like I've lost my damned mind. I'm not the right person for him because I'm female. I'm not sure if he's let himself realise it yet but he doesn't need a woman at all. No, he needs a man and for obvious reasons, I can't be that person for him.

It's not me, it's him. Literally!

Wiping the tears from my eyes, I pull my phone out of my pocket and dial my best friend.

"Hey Lori, did you do it?"

"Yes."

"How'd he take it?" Jenni asks, concern but I don't think her concern is for me funnily enough. I snort out a laugh through my tears and answer her.

"About as well as I expected him to and yet kind of better than I was expecting, all at the same time."

"Maybe he's not as unaware of his feelings as we think then?" The hope in her voice obvious.

I snort again before answering her. "No, I think he's as in the dark as he was an hour ago. I just hope eventually he realises who he truly is before he gets hurt too badly."

"Or hurts someone else too badly." She pauses. "I know you love him Lori but you did what you had to do."

"I know but that doesn't mean it doesn't hurt, nor does it mean that I wanted to hurt *him* Jenni." A sob escapes me as I hold in my tears.

"I know hun but it had to be done." She sighs and I know she doesn't have one clue what to say to me. "Where are you? I'll come meet you and we can go have a coffee."

"On a bench under a tree."

"Well, isn't that helpful on our bench and tree filled campus?" Her sarcasm filled words makes me laugh, which I'm hoping was her intention.

"I'll meet you at Joey's Café on Mayberry Street in a couple of minutes."

"Are you sure you don't want me to meet you where you are?"

"I'm sure."

"Are you saying that because you're not exactly sure where you are yourself right now?" I can't help laughing because sometimes I think this woman knows me better than I know myself.

"Maybe."

"You're hopeless, you know that right? Why didn't you meet him some-where that was familiar to you?" She scolds me, while laughing at me at the same time. When I don't answer her, she sighs. "Fine I'll meet you at Joey's but you have some explaining to do young lady."

"See you soon." I tell her, hanging up before she realises that if I don't know where I am exactly, how the hell am I going to work out how to get to Joey's.

Looking up from my phone, I look around to get my bearings and realise I'm closer to a building I recognise than I realised. Which means, I also know how to get to Joey's from here.

I take two steps in the direction I need to go when my phone chimes with a message.

Jenni: *Bitch! Don't hang up on me especially when I don't know where the fuck you are!*

Me: *I know where I am and I'll meet you at Joey's in about five minutes. I promise.*

I can't help laughing at her message and keep walking.

Jenni: *five minutes!? I thought you said you'd be there in a* couple *of minutes, now it's FIVE?!*

Me: *If you stop messaging me, I'll be there sooner*

Jenni: *Fine! I'm already here, I'll grab a table* BUT *if you're not here in FOUR minutes I'm calling campus security.*

Me: *and tell them what? I'm missing but you don't know where from?*

Jenni: *Shut up! Just get here already would ya?*

It takes me less than five minutes to get to the café and I find Jenni alone at a table meant for four. I slide into the seat opposite her, just as a waiter brings over two coffees.

"Thank you." I smile at him as he places one in front of me.

"Any time sweetheart." My smile fades a little at being called sweetheart by a guy I don't know but I nod at him anyway.

"God I hate it when they call you *sweetheart*, it's so condescending!" Jenni complains, loud enough that the waiter would have heard her as he walks away. I have to give him credit though because he doesn't turn back our way, even though he stumbles over his own feet for a second.

"Well, we'll be getting a different waiter now." I press my lips together in disapproval.

"What? Did you want to go out with him?" I shake my head, she knows that's not the case. "He should know better than to call a stranger, a *customer*, sweetheart. It's a term of endearment, not a casual, one off meeting."

"Would you rather be called ma'am?" I ask, smirking behind my hot cup of coffee as I bring it to my lips because I *know* how she's going to react to *that* suggestion.

"No! I'm not eighty years old!" I can't help it, I start laughing and I have to put my cup back down on the table. "Every time." She mutters.

"You walk in to it every time, Jenni. You need to calm down, I'm sure he didn't mean to offend you, or me for that matter." Deciding we need to change the subject before my best friend starts another rant about people being crappy human beings, I talk before she can. "So, what are you doing over semester break? It's the last one before reality hits."

"The usual." She says with a non-committal shrug. "You know."

"You can come home with me if you want." I say quietly, knowing that going home isn't an option for her. "Mum would love to see you again." I smile when Jenni smiles at the mention of my Mum.

"I wouldn't mind seeing the old girl but I have other plans."

"Like what?" Skipping over her use of the term, 'old girl' because I know she uses it to deflect her emotions over not having a home to go back to in our breaks.

"I accepted an invitation to join a group of friends at the beach. I knew you'd be going home, so I said yes already. Sorry." Jenni doesn't apologise for much, she rarely says anything she doesn't mean, so feels that there's no need.

"That's OK, you know I always go home, at least for a little while, every break. You're also welcome every time that I do, you know that, right?" I wait for her to answer me, staring at her over the rim of my cup. I know eventually she'll stop nodding and look up to answer me because she feels the weight of my stare. It gets her every time.

"I know, but I never want to overstep my welcome." She says quietly. It breaks my heart that my usually confident best friend, who will fight anyone who says she can't do something or tell her what she *should* do, has become so unsure of herself.

"You're never overstepping Jenni. Ever." I reach over to take her hand in mine. "You never have to second guess if you're welcome or not because you're always welcome."

"I know." She nods, tears building in her eyes. That is until she sniffs once and they miraculously clear up. "So, when do you head home?" She changes the subject swiftly and I know she doesn't want to talk about her anymore.

"I don't know, now that I've broken up with Logan, I kind of want to get out of here as soon as I can. I don't want to run into him around campus, I have the feeling he's going to try and win me back. Before you say anything, he didn't say that at all. He took the break up pretty well actually, better than I was expecting to be honest but I just have this weird feeling that he's going to try to 'work things out'. I think I'll talk to my professors and see if I can head home within the next day or two."

"Are you sure about that?"

'Yeah. I've handed in all my papers and all our exams are done, I don't see why I couldn't start my break a week early." I shrug my shoulders. I want to give Logan the time and distance to see that I did the right thing.

"I think you should do it. Like you said, the next few days are a waste of time and maybe giving Logan the extra time will help heal his broken heart."

I pull out my phone and send emails to my professors while Jenni keeps telling me about the trip she's going to take to the beach over the break. Before we've finished our second round of coffees and a slice of cake each, they've all responded and told me to head home. I might have told a small lie about my Mum being unwell but they don't have to know that!

Moving home

We went back to the apartment that we share after our coffees at Joey's, I packed and Jenni worked on some last minute projects that she needed to finish before she could take the next couple of weeks off to go to the beach.

When we were both done, we order in some Chinese food and settled down in front of the TV to watch one of our favourite soppy movies and ate ice cream out of the tub.

When I get up the next morning, Jenni has already left for her first class. She didn't say goodbye, it's not her style to be fair but when I go to make myself a coffee before I leave for the drive home, I find a note leaning against my favourite mug.

Hey Lori,
Have a safe trip home and tell Mumma
Stephenson I said hi and I love her.
I'll see you when you get home.
Message me when you get there!
Love Jenni xx

Instead of leaving her a note, I send her a text knowing she won't get it until after her first class.

Me: *I love you too Jenni, have fun at the beach xx*

My phone chimes almost immediately with a message.

Jenni: *Call me when you get there!*

Me: *Promise! Aren't you in class?*

Jenni: *Yeah and old man Lungren has noticed me looking at my lap so I'm going to go now, bye*

Professor Lungren *isn't* in fact an old man, which is why he knows exactly why Jenni keeps looking in her lap while he's at the front of the class, lecturing them all! All the students, male and female, call him 'old man' because he's closer to our age than any other professor on campus. Jenni, like most of the girls and some of the guys, has a crush on the poor guy and it's simply because he's *not* old enough to be out father or grandfather.

I'm still laughing at Jenni's response when my phone chimes again as I wash my empty coffee cup and put it away. Thinking it's Jenni again, I pick it up but when I look at the screen it's not Jenni's name I see.

Logan: *can we talk? Please?*

The smile drops from my face and I sigh. A big, deep, painful sigh. This right here is why I need to get away as soon as I can.

Me: *I don't think that's a good idea Logan.*

Logan: *Please? Just give me five minutes?*

Me: *fine! But you've only got a few minutes. Meet me in front of my building*

Logan: *thank you! I'll be there in five minutes*

I don't respond. I know I shouldn't have agreed to meet with him but I figured seeing as how I'm going home earlier than most of the other students, that I could give him a few minutes to say whatever it is he needed to say and then I could leave.

Moving around the apartment in a hurry, I grab everything I need and the two bags that I packed last night, then go downstairs to my car. Making sure everything is in the boot of the car, out of sight, I lean on the car and wait. I haven't been waiting long when Logan's car pulls up behind mine. He turns off the car but doesn't move, he sits in the driver's seat just looking at me.

"Are you getting out or are you just going to sit there for your few minutes?" I speak loudly but I don't yell, I can see that he had his window open so I know he heard me. I can also see him take a deep breath before he gets out of the car and leans against it. "Your minutes are ticking down."

"You have somewhere else to be?"

"I do actually."

"Where are you going?"

"It's none of your business, Logan, we're no longer together."

"I can't ask where you're going anymore, not even as a friend, Lori? You *did* say we could stay friends you know."

"I know I did but we broke up yesterday Logan, today is probably too soon to be calling in our 'friendship' so that you can find out my plans."

"You're right, I'm sorry."

"What is it you wanted to say, Logan? I really do have somewhere to be." There's no schedule set in stone or anything but I'd like to get driving sooner, rather than later.

"I just wanted to know, are you sure?"

"That I want to break up?"

"Yes." He nods, and I can see the honest sadness on his face. I love this guy, I truly do and I don't want to upset him but this isn't doing either of us any good.

"Logan."

"Please, I need to know."

"Yes Logan, I am one hundred percent certain that this is the right thing to do. I am not the right person for you." I take a breath and see that he's about to speak, but I hold my hand up to stop him before he can. "I love you Logan and I know you *think* you love me but honestly, I'm not the right person for you and if you're honest with yourself, you know it too. We *both* know it Logan, it doesn't mean that we can't have some love for each other but it's a friendship kind of love. You're like a brother to me, the brother I never had, you know?"

"OK." He nods, his hands digging into the front pockets of his jeans. "I know you're right Lori, I'm just, confused I guess because if I can't make it work with you, knowing how much I care about you, then I don't know how to make it work with anyone." He's wrong, he's just not looking in the right places but once he does, he's going to find the perfect person for him to love and to be loved by. I hope we're still friends when that happens because I want to see him happy. I push off my car and walk towards him and I sigh once again when I see his body stiffen. When I say body, I don't mean his cock gets hard at the thought of me touching him, no I mean he gets tense *because* I'm going to touch him.

"Logan, when you look in the right place, you're going to find the right love but we both know that isn't me." I kiss him lightly on the cheek, and tap his chest with my fingers, right over his heart. "You are worth loving Logan Drake and one day, someone will love you so hard it will repair you."

"I didn't know I was broken." He laughs uneasily.

"You're not really to be fair, I think you just have some things you need to think about and you can't do them if we're together. Not to mention, I think we're better off as friends and I think in time, you're going to see and understand that." I lay another light kiss on his cheek and turn away to get in my car.

As I open the door, I hear him move behind me and when I get comfortable in the seat, he closes the door for me and I smile at him. "Thank you, Logan, you're very sweet." I start the car and start pull out of the carpark.

"Say hi to your Mum for me." I laugh and wave out the window but I keep driving. When I look in the rearview mirror he's still standing there, leaning against his car and watching me drive away.

When I get to my Mum's a couple of hours later, she greets me on the front porch as I pull all my stuff out of the car.

"You know I love you, Sweetie but I can't help thinking a couple of things here. One, you're here a little earlier than I expected, by about a week and two, it looks like you're planning on staying for a few weeks."

"Hey Mum." I say as I walk up the front steps and kiss her on the cheek before walking past her to go inside.

"You're not going to explain why it looks like you're moving back home?" She follows me to my room that has barely changed since I moved out almost four years ago.

"I didn't know that I had to have a reason to come home for a few weeks over break."

"You don't, normally but this is sudden and you didn't even tell me you were coming."

"Am I interrupting something?" I freeze as I dump the bags on the floor of my old bedroom, I *really* don't want to be witness to anything like a booty call for my *Mother*!

"Ohh Sweetie, we don't call them booty calls at my age, they're simply no strings attached relationships." She cackles with laughter as a shiver runs down my spine just *thinking* about my mum having a man on speed dial for these things. I'm not saying she *can't* have that kind of relationship with someone if that's what she wants, I just don't want to know about it. "Speaking of, how's that gorgeous young man of yours? Will he be joining you here at some point? I'd love to have him here, he's a real sweetheart of a man, very kind."

"We broke up."

"Ohh I'm sorry Sweetie, now I feel like I was very insensitive. I know you liked him." She's not wrong, I did, I still do.

"I still do but he's not the right guy for me, that's all there is to it."

"Sometimes I worry that you're just a little bit too, selective, shall we say. You know not everyone is like your father. Most men stick around and help out when they knock their girlfriends or wives up. Just because yours didn't, doesn't mean none of them will."

"I know that Mumma. Logan and I just weren't the right fit together, that's all."

"If you're sure?" She doesn't seem convinced but that's all I've got for her in this moment.

"I am Mumma, believe me."

"Well, OK but only because you don't seem too upset by it all. When did he break up with you?"

"He didn't, I broke up with him and it was yesterday."

"*You* broke up with him? Wow!" She says, following me out of the room and back out to my car, where I grab the rest of my things out and lock it up. Not that I'm worried about anyone stealing it, it's a small town, someone would notice I wasn't driving it.

"Why do you say it like that?"

"Like what Sweetie?"

"Like you're surprised that I was the one who did it."

"Because I am?" It's more a of a question than her telling me a fact. "I just know how much you liked him, Lori and I'm surprised is all."

"I know Mumma and you're right, I did and I still do like him. He's a great guy but I'm not the person for him, which means he's not the person for me. There's no point wasting any more time, his or mine, on a relationship that can't go any further."

"So, that's that then? No more Logan to come visit me?" Her pout is both adorable and tragic at the same time, which I have to say is quite the feat.

"Sorry to disappoint you Mumma but no, no more visits from Logan Drake." I kiss her cheek again and lead her out of my room and into the kitchen so that we can have a coffee, a snack and catch up a little.

A FEW WEEKS LATER, just before I was due to return to school, I was wishing that I hadn't closed the door on our friendship by not answering any of the messages Logan sent me after our last conversation.

I'd heard on the grapevine and by that I mean Jenni, that Logan had most assuredly moved on from us and not in the way I'd hoped.

Either way, I didn't feel like it was the right time to tell him that he was going to be a Dad!

I spent most of my time at home feeling unwell but managed to hide it from my Mum for most of the time. At least I thought I had until one day, about two weeks into my visit she told me we were going into town for lunch and then dropped me off at the clinic and told me to tell the doctor that I'd been sick for two weeks straight.

When I walked back out of the clinic with a bunch of pamphlets full of information about pregnancy and babies, she took one look at my shellshocked face and helped me get in the car, before driving me home. Neither of us said a word on that drive but when we got inside and I broke down in tears, my Mum came to the rescue, just as she always had since I was a kid.

"We'll deal with this together Sweetie. You won't be on your own, I'll help you both, I promise." I nodded into her chest as I blubbered and made a snotty mess on her clean top. "I take it there's no chance you're going to tell Logan about this?"

"No, I don't think he's in the right place for this. I don't want to force him into anything and I know he'll want to do what he perceives to be the right thing and I can't let him do that. To any of us."

"It's your choice, obviously, but I think he deserves to know."

"I know and I agree. When I think the time is right, I promise I will tell him, now just isn't that time."

"OK." My Mum smiles and agrees with me, but I can see in her eyes that she's not completely on board with me not telling Logan about our baby and giving *him* the chance to make the decision for himself but I know I can't do that to any of us. It just doesn't seem fair.

In retrospect, I know it was the wrong decision, but at the time it seemed like the best thing for all of us. Instead I left University, and went back to my home town to live with my Mum.

Having a baby

Here's the thing, never in a million years did I ever think I would be telling anyone that I was having a baby. Not before I'd finished university and worked for a few years as an accountant but here we are and it's one of the biggest issues of living back home.

It's difficult to have any secrets in a small town and I hate feeling like I've disappointed my Mum.

The one thing I can never and will never regret, is having you Savannah. You were everything I never knew I needed at the time.

My pregnancy, while not exactly without its issues, it was still a relative breeze compared to what some women go through. The swollen ankles, water retention and the constant need to know exactly where the closest toilet was at *all* times, no matter where I was, were all small potatoes.

Over the six months after I found out I was pregnant, Logan messaged me. The first few months he was consistent and persistent. According to Jenni, he kept finding her and asking where I was and if I was OK. Then he started begging her to tell him that I was OK. Jenni, in all her snarky best never gave him more than, 'it's none of your business' or 'she doesn't want to talk to you' for answers, amongst other replies that I'm not sure you want to read about what your Aunt Jen said to your Dad!

Logan, as a testament to his patience and integrity, didn't give your Aunt Jen too much of a break until in the end, Jen told him that I had moved to another school to be with a guy I'd met right after we broke up. I'm glad I didn't have to see his face when she told him that, I think it might have broken my heart but at the time, we did what we thought was for the best.

Your grandma and Jen helped me through the pregnancy and birth as best as they could. Jen finished up school and moved closer to us to help out. What you don't know, is the nights that Grandma stayed up with you so that I could sleep. Or the mornings she got up early so that I could sleep in. Or all the millions of little things that she did that I couldn't even explain to you now but they helped in so many ways back then. She loved having you around the house, I think it brought a light and excitement back into her life that she hadn't realised was missing, before she passed away.

Bringing you home from the hospital was an event and an experience in itself. I know I couldn't have made it through without your grandma helping me, us really, in those first few days, weeks and months.

Of course, your Aunt Jenni helped out as much as she could too but she knew less about babies than I did, so it was a true case of the blind leading the blind, with the two of us together. Thank heavens for your grandmother! Like me, Jenni learnt as we went along and I hope, now that you're with your Dad, that she can still be a huge part of your life. It would be a shame if she isn't but I would also understand.

Aunt Jenni was an absolute godsend your entire life. From the moment I found out I was pregnant that woman has stood by me and you without question. Jen was my birthing partner and came to every class I needed another person to attend with me.

She was there when you were born and was the first person to hold you. I'm pretty sure that the midwife thought we were a couple and neither one of us ever corrected her! It was definitely a fair assumption seeing as how she was at every check-up that she could attend and every birthing class *and* in the delivery room. She was also the one who brought us both home from the hospital.

Grandma was there for everything as well but I guess, Jen stepped into the place where the partner normally goes. At the time, it didn't feel weird for either of us. Once I started to get sick and I was in my last few weeks, I realised the sacrifice that Jen made for us. She didn't have a partner or kids of her own because she'd spent so much of her life and time with us.

Life at home when we got there, was just so busy that I never took the time to think. I was very grateful that she was around as often as she was and told her more times than not that she needed to get her own life. We had grandma and we would be fine without her for a while but Jenni always insisted that it wasn't a hardship to be around either of us, including grandma!

Your first few years were the same as everyone else's I guess. Eating, crapping, sleeping, crying and growing. It felt like every time we got into a routine, and things settled down, you decided to change the routine and cause chaos for a while again. Grandma told me that every new baby was the same and that one day, in the very distant future I might feel like I'd have any kind of real sleep again!

Every day was a new adventure and even though some days I would have relished having the same adventure as the day before, I never once wished that we weren't together on the adventure. Though, I did wish that you had a larger family unit, specifically your dad around but I also knew that was going to take some effort on my part. The four of us were a very tight family unit though and there was nothing we couldn't count on each other for. I'm pretty sure the four of us could have taken on the world together and some days, it felt like we did.

Grandma was a godsend as well. She did a lot of the night feeds so that I could sleep and took you out for afternoon strolls and later playdates so that I could have time to myself. Grandma was there for us in ways that I never even realised until after she was gone.

The thing is, no-one ever really tells you just how hard having a baby will be. I think all women realise that giving *birth* is going to hurt but I don't think any of them realise that the truth is, in a weird and twisted way, that physical pain is the easiest part. Being responsible for another human being is hard work! From the minute a baby is born, they're at our complete mercy. They need us to feed them, keep them clean and warm or cool, whatever the case may be. Let me tell you, it's not for the faint of heart, that's for certain! I don't think many mums or parents tell you the truth before you've had kids yourself and there seems to be something fundamentally wrong with that fact, although I doubt anyone would actually listen to the advice anyway. We always think things are going to be different for us. We'll do better, be better, *our* baby will and be perfect! We are *wrong!* Nothing could be further from the truth.

Do I think *you* were and still are perfect? Oh hell yes but you're *my* baby and even when you're in your 40's with a child or children of your own, you'll *always* be *my* baby! Nothing in the world will ever change that! Whether I'm there with you or not, this will always be the truth.

The first six years of your life were a *huge* learning curve for all involved. Even Grandma had to relearn things and I can tell you, that didn't always go down so well. She had more than a few 'discussions' with healthcare professionals along the way. Amusing for me to watch, not so much for the professionals defending the new 'childrearing ways'. As you know, Grandma was a stickler for the way things 'used to be' and I felt sorry for the people who told her that her ideas were old fashioned. I had to step in to stop the arguments a number of times, sometimes I wasn't sure whose side I would have taken if I'd been asked to, so I just played the role of peacekeeper and made everyone agree to disagree.

Grandma and I didn't always agree on things but she was always there for us. She had more than a few sharp words for Jenni as well. They loved each other so much but when it came to you, they *both* thought they knew what was best, both forgetting that I happened to be your mother and was the one who ultimately got to make the choices. Not saying I didn't appreciate their help *or* their suggestions but it wasn't always easy when the two of them disagreed on something.

Take getting you into Kinder! Oh my lord! Anyone would have thought we were signing you up to University and you needed to go to the best of the best. At four years old, all I really needed was for you to feel safe and learn things along the way. Kinder doesn't make your career and so I made the choice without telling them. I'm not even sure I told them when your first day was, I think we just got ready for the day and when they *both* asked where we were off to, I told them then. You might have to ask Aunt Jenni for that story because my fuzzy brain just can't join the dots right now.

Then one day, I came home before picking you up and I found Grandma, well you don't need to know the details but she passed away that day. I've thought about it every day since, wishing that I'd gone home earlier but the doctors and paramedics reassured me that her heart attack was instant. I wouldn't have changed the outcome in the slightest.

It still left an ache in my heart that she was alone when she took her last breath.

I don't ever want you to have similar regrets. If things went to plan, you got to say your goodbye.

Cancer

A few months after my mum passed away, I couldn't sleep enough and I wasn't hungry. I thought I was still grieving. I *thought* it would get better, that I would be fine. I *thought* it was because I was worrying about where we would live. Being an only child meant there weren't any siblings to fight over possessions, which helped things move faster.

Six months of listening to Jenni tell me off and demand that I go see a doctor who gave us the answer to why I was feeling like absolute crap.

Cancer.

Jenni, once again, came to the rescue. She'd already been staying with us most days and commuting to work from here. Once I got the diagnosis, she moved in. I didn't get the chance to argue with her, to tell that she didn't need to put her life on hold for me, for us, she just did it. There was no discussion, she went home one day and came back two days later with all her stuff and told me that she'd given up her apartment, packed up all her things and she was moving in.

When I asked her about work, all she told me was, 'I can work from wherever I am and believe me, we won't starve'. I guess it was supposed to be reassuring but it really wasn't. Til the day I left this world, I had no freaking idea what that woman did to earn money. In the end, I'm not sure I wanted to know. She told me so many different things over the years, I often wondered if she'd told me the truth wrapped up in a myriad of lies. She was right about one thing though, we never did starve or need for anything.

It was around this time that I seriously started to try to get in contact with Logan. I was trying to find him on social media prior to that but I wasn't having much luck. The man was nowhere to be found! I remembered that his parents had a vineyard and winery, so I decided to look it up.

That's how I found Drake Wines and obviously, that's also how I found Logan Drake. I just couldn't get him to return my emails, messages or phone calls.

Instead of concentrating on getting Logan to talk to me, I put all my efforts into my treatments and loving you, Savannah. At least, I tried to when the chemo didn't make me too sick to get out of bed.

I know that you don't know the details of my treatment and I'm not sure how much you want to know now or how much I want to share with you but I want to be honest with you.

Jenni was once again my saviour. She was there for you when I couldn't be and there for me when I needed her, without question. She just seemed to know what was needed and she did it.

Unfortunately, the treatments didn't work and I was given weeks, maybe months to live. Jenni and I sat up until all hours for weeks discussing, what would happen when I was gone. She kept insisting that she would take you in, that you guys keep living in the house and nothing would have to change for you but we both knew that wasn't healthy.

Jenni needed to get on with her own life. She sacrificed her life for too long to help me and I couldn't let her continue doing it. She needed to find love and her own way in the world.

We argued, we cried, we talked and then, we cried some more. Poor Jenni, she understood why I had to do what I was about to do but she didn't like it one bit.

We sold everything, including the house, so that you would have a nest egg for later in life and then we went on a road trip. Our destination, Drake Wines and making Logan talk to me one way or another.

Jenni wanted to come with me, always in protection mode. I wasn't supposed to be driving, she reasoned but when I explained that I didn't want you to meet Logan until I'd had a chance to talk to him first and that you couldn't, and shouldn't, stay at the hotel alone, she gave in. Not without reservations but she let me go.

Pulling up to the restaurant on the property turned me in a bundle of nerves. I was fine on the drive over, I'd had all my meds and I was feeling good, not great but good. Driving was distracting enough to settle my nerves. Not that I was nervous about seeing Logan, I knew he wouldn't actually be nasty, I was aware though that he might not be very happy to see me. I had, after all, effectively walked out of his life without explanation and as it turns out, kept a massive secret from him for all these years. In my defence, I'd tried to contact him earlier and he just didn't answer.

I sat in my car for way too long once I pulled up and I started getting a few weird looks, which meant it was either time to bite the bullet and get out of the car, or head back to the hotel. I knew if I didn't get out of the car, I wouldn't have the guts to come back again and I wasn't here for me. I was here for you, Savannah. You were going to need your dad more than ever, which meant that I had to pull up my big girl undies and do what needed to be done.

I made my way inside Vines, the bistro on the Drake Wines property, it was busy and noisy in an easy, comfortable kind of way. There's a table of older ladies laughing loudly and a young man who looks so remarkably like Logan, that he has to be his younger brother. I make a beeline for him and get cut short by a waitress asking me if she can help me. I smile back and say, 'no thank you', and keep moving towards Caleb Drake. I know his name because I saw them all on the Drake Wines website. I also know that the other guy sitting with him is his brother in law, Brady Harris.

"Caleb?" I ask, as I reach their table and I feel the whole room still. The waitress who spoke to me as I walked in moves to stand behind Caleb protectively.

"Yes." The guy I pegged as Caleb says, standing up and holding his hand out to me. "Can I help you? Have we met before?" His face crinkles in confusion and I can't help laughing. He's very adorable!

"No, Caleb, we've never met before. I *do* know your brother though and I was wondering if he was around?" I know he got married yesterday and I'm really hoping that Logan and his husband haven't already gone on their honeymoon, otherwise, I'm going to have to wait another week or more and I'm not sure I have that kind of time left.

"You know Logan?" Caleb asks, looking shocked and I laugh again.

"It's not like he doesn't know other people of the human variety, Caleb." Brady, who stands up and offers me his hand.

"Hi, I'm Brady, Logan and Caleb's brother in law. How do you know Logan?" Brady asks, sending Caleb a weird look that I just don't understand.

"I went to university with him and there's something important I need to talk to him about." It's all the information I can or will offer, before talking to

Logan and his husband. "I realise he got married yesterday but I was hoping that he hadn't left for his honeymoon yet."

"What do you need to tell him?" Brady asks and while I know that he's trying to protect Logan, I'm not going to tell these two and anyone listening in the bistro, about our daughter. Logan deserves to know before anyone else.

"Nothing I want to share here." I glare at him, with everything I can muster. "I need to talk to Logan. Alone."

"Well, he's not going to be alone." Brady tells me. "He has a husband now."

"I know." I nod. "I know you all live here on the property. If you could just point me in the right direction, I'll be on my way."

"Let me message him and he can meet you here." Caleb suggests.

"I'd rather talk to him in private but thanks for the offer." I smile at him gently.

"If you go back outside and walk up the driveway, you'll see his place on the left." Caleb directs.

"Caleb." Brady growls, his disapproval obvious.

"Does she *look* like a serial killer to you?" He asks his brother in law.

"What the hell does a serial killer *look* like, Caleb?" Brady growls in response. "Serial killers look like everybody else, that's why they get away with literal murder, you idiot."

Taking the opportunity to sneak out of the bistro while the two men argue, I made for the front door, only to be stopped by the same woman who stopped me on the way in.

"*Are* you a serial killer?" She asks, her arms crossed over her chest and a scowl on her face. I look at her chest to find a name badge.

"Leila, is it?" She gave me one swift nod. "No, I'm not a serial killer, I promise. I'm not here to do any harm to anyone. I need to talk to Logan and his husband about something, that's all. I don't want to hurt anyone."

"Jules."

"I'm sorry?"

"His husband's name. It's Jules, well Julian to you, I guess."

"Thank you." I say as she steps aside, opening the door for me.

"Don't hurt them." She warns. "There are a lot of people who will hunt you down if you do."

I smiled at her, happy in the knowledge that when you come to live here, you're going to be surrounded by people who will love and protect you as well because I made very sure that Logan will accept you, which means the people who love him will too.

I take a deep breath and make my way towards the house that Caleb indicated, steeling myself for the conversation that is ahead of me.

Telling Logan

When I got to Logan's door, I could hear laughter and talking. I realised I was about to be the one to burst their bubble of happiness! I took a steeling breath and knock.

"Nice to know that you can learn from your mistakes, Caleb." I hear from inside, I would know that voice anywhere and he's happy. Happier than I've heard him.

"Hey Caleb, thanks for knocking this time –" His laughter trails off when he realises it's not his brother but his ex-girlfriend. "Lori?"

"Yeah, not Caleb, sorry to disappoint you, Logan." I laugh nervously but with what I hope is a warm smile. "I guess he's still the annoying little brother, hmm?"

"Umm what?" Poor Logan, he looks completely confused.

"Well, you said as you opened the door that you're glad he's learned his lesson. I'm guessing he walks in unannounced and catches you in positions no-one wants to be caught in. Am I right?"

"Ahh yes, you are, actually." He stammered out. "What – what are you doing here?" He looked over his shoulder and I can only assume he's looking for his new husband.

"Can I come in please? We really need to talk and I think this is something your husband might be interested in hearing as well." The shock on his face that I recognise that he's married and to a man, would be amusing if I didn't find it a little sad that he thought that I would judge him for it.

"Sure, come on in." Logan steps to the side to let me into the house. I take in their home and realise that it suits him perfectly. It's modern but has enough soft touches that you can see his soft centre. Perhaps those softer edges are Julian's touches but I know that Logan Drake is softer than he looks.

"Congratulations, by the way." I tell him, as I get further into his home and came face to face with the man who must be his husband. "Hi." I smile at him, he's gorgeous in a very proper way. "I'm Lori."

"Hi Lori, I'm Jules." He smiles warmly back at me and holding his hand out for me to shake. I like him right away.

"My husband. Jules that is, he's my husband. We got married yesterday." Logan stumbles and I try not to laugh at him because I imagine that me showing up on his doorstep has definitely caught him off guard. It is fun to watch him stumble around though because the Logan I remember, was always Mr Confident. He knew what to say, when to say and how to say it. He always managed to make people comfortable and I never could work out how.

"I know. Congratulations to you both." I smile at them but I can't help the smirk that I feel on my face as I watch Logan wrap an arm around Julian's waist, pulling him in close to his side. I don't know whether he's protecting Julian or himself, or if he's trying to tell me to back off. "I'm so glad you're happy Logan. I'm very happy that you found the right person to be with and found yourself along the way."

"Thank you." He replies and there are a few awkward beats of silence until Julian offers me a drink and I ask for a water, wishing that I had gotten one in Vines when I was there just a few minutes ago.

While Julian gets drinks, Logan offers me a seat in the living room, which I gratefully take. My medication is starting to wear off and I know I need to get to the reason I'm here, otherwise my illness is going to be the spotlight that I don't want it to be just yet.

"It's really good to see you, Logan." I smiled as I sit down in one of the comfiest looking armchairs I think I've ever seen, leaving the couch for Logan and Jules to sit on together.

"It's a surprise to see you, Lori, I have to admit." He says it with a smile, one that I remember and have really missed.

I can't help laughing at Julian telling Logan to use his manners and joking that he isn't quite house broken quite yet but I'm not even close to offended. I know Logan and I don't believe he's changed too much over the years. Perhaps he's gotten a little more surly and world weary but he's still the same man underneath.

When I mention that, Julian seems to withdraw a little and I can't help wondering if I offended him somehow by hinting that I know his husband better than he does. Logan reaching over and taking the bottle of water out of my shaking hand to open it for me as if we're still comfortable with each other as we were back then, just over eight years ago.

Telling them that I have cancer wasn't easy. It's never easy dropping that little bomb on anyone but dropping it on your ex-boyfriend and his new husband when you haven't seen said ex for almost a decade is pretty awkward. I've had time to come to terms with my diagnosis, Logan hasn't and I know it takes time but we don't have time for him to get used to the idea that I'm dying.

"I'm sorry, Lori." Logan says simply and I know he means it because I've never known him to say things that he didn't mean.

"Right then. I think I'll leave you two to talk." Julian gets up to leave us alone but I stop him.

I ask Julian to stay, if that's OK with both of them because this is going to affect them both. I'm not asking them a favour as such but I am effectively giving them an instant family. I'm just hoping that they accept you, Savannah as their family as easily I think they will. I *know* that Logan wouldn't be with anyone who is a bad person but that doesn't mean that they want a family, especially an instant what the likes of which I'm dishing them up.

"I have a daughter, Logan." I blurt out. Poor Logan, he looks so confused.

"I'm happy for you but what does that have to do with me?"

The guy, he looks confused and I know I'm going to have to explain it to him in black and white. "She's almost *eight* Logan. *Think* about it!"

"You mean ...?" He stutters and I know he's suddenly done the maths and put two and two together.

"Yes." I confirm.

"Ohhhhh." Is all he manages when it finally registers with him. "Oh fuck me!"

"Well, yeah, that's how it happened." I smile, trying to soften the blow that I'd just delivered. "I need your help." I say quietly.

"Anything." Logan doesn't even hesitate and I know I'm doing the right thing. Not that I didn't before but now that he knows and we're talking about this, face to face, I feel relieved and comforted all at once.

A peace came over me in that moment. Logan and Julian, they're going to help me, us and they're going to be wonderful Dads to you, my darling, Savannah.

Moving In

I felt like an intruder sitting there listening to Julian trying to understand the significance of your age, Savannah. The dawning realisation on his face was something else.

"So, who is your daughter's father?" He asked, slowly, looking me in the eye.

"Are you sure?" Logan asks me and I nod once to confirm that yes, I certainly am. "One hundred percent? Because I'm not explaining this to Jules only for this to not be what I think it is."

"I couldn't be more sure, Logan." I sigh. "I know this isn't the best timing but you left me no other choice when you didn't respond to any other communication. I'm running out of time."

Then he explains the timeline to his husband and I'm not really sure how he's going to react. I barely know the man but he seems like an exceptionally kind person. I could tell that he knew about me, which was reassuring in a weird way to know that Logan had told him about his past. That he hadn't hidden that part of him from the man he loves and is committed to.

I stand up to leave, to give them both some time to get absorb and discuss the news I just dropped on them both. I'd had a card with my details already written out before I came out here, so I handed that over to Logan, who took it from me without a word. "We're staying in town, so I can be here within twenty or so minutes if you want to chat." I tell them quietly, not wanting to shatter the weird silence that is now in the room.

"No!" Logan says. That one word said sharply, causes me to stop in my tracks.

"I'm sorry? What do you mean, no?" I'm confused because I have no idea what the hell he's saying no to. No to you being his daughter? No to me leaving? No to us staying in a hotel?

"Stay. You'll stay here." He pauses before asking, "What do you mean, us?"

"Jenni, Savannah and I are staying at a hotel in town, not too far from here." I tell him, thinking that will make him happy, knowing that we're close by.

"Savannah." He said your name like you were a princess and I notice that Julian is wondering how the hell Logan would know that I didn't name you Jenni. "That's her name?"

"Yes, Savannah Rae." Then he asked to meet you as if he thought after all of this, that I might say no. He also asked about Jenni, wondering if she didn't in fact want to take his life because he left me alone with a child. Not that your dad knew you existed before I arrived here today, so Jenni has no real reason for her resentment towards him. To be honest, it's not something I've ever understood.

Then he asked me if Jenni knew that I was pregnant when he was asking about me, wanting to talk to me. I have to admit that not only did she know but she didn't tell him at my request. Watching the hurt flit across his face is hard but I know I did the right thing.

"I wanted you to be happy, Logan." I explain, hoping like hell he can understand my reasoning for not telling him back then. "And look at you! You've found the happiness you deserve. A man and a happiness you wouldn't have found if I had told you about my pregnancy." I know without a doubt that your dad would have done everything in his power to help us both. He would have finished school, married me and we would have lived as a family but he wouldn't have been happy. Not as happy as he is now, married to the love of his life, anyway. I have no doubt he would have been happy with you in his life, no matter the circumstances, which is also why I'm here now.

"Tell your friend, Jenni, is it? To pack up your things, you're coming to stay here." Julian says, breaking his silence. "I know it might be too soon and I get that it might be too overwhelming for Miss Savannah to meet her Dad, as well as me and the rest of the family but you can't stay in a hotel. I won't allow it. You're not well and we can help. Can't we, Logan?"

"Of course, Lori and Savannah come first." His voice is cold, distant and I wasn't expecting that.

I try to tell them that it's not necessary but Julian insists and then leaves in a rush to see about getting the cottage he says we can live in cleaned up. I can see the panic on Logan's face and I try telling him that it's not necessary. We're fine where we are for now but he won't take no for an answer and asks me if

I'm Ok to go up to Vines and wait for him there. I agree, simply because I can see that he needs to go and find Julian so that they can talk this whole situation through. I don't think either of them will change their minds about having you around Savannah, it's not in their natures but its this is a big deal. Not only did I announce to your dad and his *new* husband that he's a father but I also basically asked them to take you in after I'm gone. That's a lot for anyone to take in.

When I enter Vines, Caleb is still in there, sitting alone at a table this time with his laptop and a coffee.

"Is it OK if I sit here?" I ask, not wanting to assume he wants company but he looks up from the screen with a welcoming smile on his face.

"Of course it is! Any ex-girlfriend of my brothers is a friend of mine." I can't help laughing at his cheeky grin.

"You were trouble as a kid, weren't you, Caleb?"

"I might have been but I've matured. Now I'm just fun to be around." I can't help laughing at him. "Did you want something to eat? Drink? I can get Sara to bring you a cake or something or Georgie to make you a coffee of your choice. Believe me, she makes the best in the world."

"With a glowing recommendation like, I feel bad about saying no." I smile at him because it's really hard not to, he's such a charming young man. He's definitely going to be the fun uncle who takes you on an adventure as often as he can.

"Is there anything I can get for you?" His sincerity is touching.

"I wouldn't mind an iced water, if it's no trouble."

"It's no trouble at all." He says, getting up from his chair and walking over to the counter and then ducking behind it, he gets my water and quickly brings it back to the table. "How did it go? Talking to Logan?" I know he's fishing for information but I'm going to leave it to Logan and Julian to tell their families about us, that's not up to me. I don't get the chance to answer him because a couple comes up to the table to talk to Caleb, who introduces me.

"Oh, you're Logan's ex and baby Mumma huh?" The man, Gavin I think his name was.

"His what?" Caleb asks a little too loudly.

"Yeah, they have a daughter together." Gavin announces and his wife tells him off.

"Daughter! You've got a daughter together?" Again, Caleb's surprise makes his voice louder than I'm comfortable with and I swear you can hear a pin drop in Vines and that's the moment that your dad and Julian decide to walk in the door.

I drink my ice water while listening to Caleb, Gavin and Logan discussing and explaining what just happened. Then, Gavin and his wife take their leave with a round of goodbyes and congratulations to the newly married couple.

My medications are starting to wear off, knowing this, I want to get to my car so that I can get a new round into me so that I can get myself back to the hotel. Back to you but your dad has a very different idea. When Caleb brings up the fact that if Logan doesn't tell their sister himself about you and I, then there will be hell to pay, I sit and watch as he sends her a message, pulling together a family meeting. I've never *had* to call a 'family meeting', there wasn't enough people to meet *with* and I love seeing this part of him.

When I stand up to leave, I assumed that your dad didn't want me there when he spoke to your aunt about us for the first time, I feel a little dizzy and unwell.

"Do you need something?" Logan asks me.

"My meds. I left them in the car." Caleb asks for my keys and he heads out to get them for me.

Logan and Julian seem to exchange a conversation without words and then they're on either side of me, walking out of Vines and towards my car. I'm grateful for their support. Leila, the waitress appears next to us at the car with a nice cold bottle of water so that I can take the pills. Then we slowly make our way to Makenna's house.

The next thing I know, Logan's swept me up in his arms and he's carrying me to the house, I wrap my arms around his neck and snuggle into his chest, even as I tell him that I'm not his to look after anymore and he assures me, that as the mother of his child, I *am* his responsibility.

"Mother of his child? What the hell is going on here?" A female voice, that I can only assume is his sister asks. Logan introduces me and tells her that we're moving into the cottage that Gavin and Jilly just vacated. Without hesitating, Brady offers to come and help collect you and Jenni, as well as our belongings.

The decision made, Caleb announces that he's brought my car up to the house, saying that he'll follow us in his truck with Brady, back to the hotel. I don't have the energy to argue and I know that Jenni isn't going to be happy but I think it might be for the best. My baby girl will get the chance to get to know her family while still being comfortable with us around as well.

When we hit the road, I pull my phone out of my bag and see a few messages from Jenni wanting to know how it's going. Instead of messaging, I call her.

"What's going on? Are you OK? Do I need to come do some damage to Logan Drake?" I can't help laughing at her rush of questions.

"Everything is fine, better than fine actually. You don't need to harm Logan in anyway. I promise." I glance Logan's way and see the small smirk on his lips. "We're on our way to the hotel, actually."

"What do you mean we? I knew I shouldn't have let you drive yourself over there. Please tell me that Logan at least insisted that he drive you back?"

"He did actually but that's not the only reason he's driving me back." I hedge, simply because I'm not sure how to tell her about the decision to stay out at Drake Wines.

"I'm glad he's still a decent person. It makes me feel better about, well you know, the whole situation."

"Can make sure all our stuff is packed up?" I close my eyes, steeling myself for her questions.

"Why? Why would I pack up our stuff? I thought we were staying here for a while?" She doesn't say it but what she means is, before I need to go to hospice care.

"We're moving into a cottage on the Drake property." I say in a rush.

"I'm sorry, what did you just say?"

"Look, this will be easier for everyone. OK, maybe not *you* but think about Savannah." I feel guilty for bringing you into it but it's the perfect way to get Jenni to agree to anything, all I have to tell her is that it's the best thing for you. She gives in every time. "This way, we're all close by and she can be with us while getting to know Logan, Julian and their family."

The silence on the other end of the line worries me but I know I need to give her a minute or two to warm up to the idea. I know that she'll come around because she knows that it's in your best interest to do things this way.

"OK."

"OK?" I ask, not sure what she's agreeing with.

"OK. I'll get everything organised here."

"Are you sure?"

"Of course. You're right. It's the perfect situation for Savannah. It will help her to get comfortable with them while we're both still around to make sure she has a safe place to land." The words she left unspoken were the things that neither of us want to talk about yet.

She meant while *I'm* still here.

My final days

Being that Jenni was a little more willing to move into a cottage on Drake Wines than I was expecting, it went a lot smoother than I was expecting.

I watched as Julian made the effort to get to know all of us. He included Jenni and myself in every decision that was to be made, whether it was meals, a cleaning routine and most importantly, my medical care. He was kind and gentle with everyone, it didn't matter what we were doing or what reason a person was on the property, he took it all in stride and tried to make it as easy and painless as possible.

I adored him for it.

He also sat with *me* for hours. Hours and hours that man spent with me, getting to know me and asking me to tell him all about life. My life before you, my life *with* you and everything in between. We laughed and we cried together but we also had a lot of moments of pure, unadulterated peace, where we just sat. We sat out on what I guess you would call the back porch of the small cottage that was made for visitors and instead became our home, to look out over the vineyard and just be. He was the only one that really let me do that. Just breathe, in and out and *be* in the moment. Everyone else expected something of me or from me. I'm not complaining, not at all, I wanted that as well but it was nice to just, sit.

Your dad was amazing as well. He set up hospice care at home, in the cottage for me when he realised just how far advanced the cancer was. He never made a decision about any of it without consulting me or your Aunt Jenni and for just that alone, I could see the ice melting between them.

We chose a new school for you together. All four of us sitting down to decide what would be the best for you. We didn't always agree on things, believe me, your Dad and Jenni still argued over every other decision that had to be made *but* the heat in the disagreements seemed to be less flame and more smoke. Which made it fun to watch, rather than causing me to wonder if they might actually murder each other before we could get you settled. I do believe that Julian had a lot to do with that too. At least I believe he talked your dad around to behaving and getting to know Jenni before losing his temper with her.

That step-father of yours is a true gem. He is the perfect partner for your dad, I see it with such clarity as I watch them together in my last days. He supports and loves Logan in a way that I know I never could have and it makes my heart happy that I walked away when I did. I still wish that all of this, you meeting your dad, happened sooner but life is what we make of it and I'm taking absolute joy in watching the three of you together. The bond that you're building is incredible and I know I can rest easy now, knowing without a doubt that you will be loved and adored forever. Even after I'm gone.

Along with your dad and step-father, you gained a set of grandparents that adore you beyond belief! Julian's parents have accepted you and taken you on as if you were just always here, a part of their family. Do I need to mention your aunt and uncles? I see that connection you have with Caleb and I understand *why*. He is one charming man and he's the young, fun uncle. Let's not forget Makenna and Brady because I see Makenna taking her time to get to know you and Brady's being just so sweet, they're going to make amazing parents.

I'm grateful that Aunt Makenna and Uncle Brady let you help them out with all the things for the baby. Hopefully, that new arrival will help you all see that life and death come hand in hand. That out of the bad, there always comes something good.

My grandfather had a lot of strange sayings but the one that stuck with me, the one I found more comforting than strange was that for every loss, a new life was born. Not with the intention to replace but to replenish the heart and soul. So that those left behind could find love in a world that can be a hard place to find that unconditional love.

Watching everyone pull together and pull you and Jenni into their fold really, truly warms my heart. It proves my grandfather's theory of finding unconditional love for those left behind. I know that you'll be well taken care of and that means that I can relax.

They've brought me into their warm embrace as well and I will never forget that. I want *you* to never forget just how welcoming they've been. I could have never dreamed of a more perfect family for you to grow up in.

The fact is though, I always knew that once Logan knew he was a dad, that he was *your* dad, he would accept that and *you* without hesitation. Jenni might have had her reservations but I didn't have one. Not even half a one and when I found out that he had gotten married, I knew that the man that he married would welcome you into their lives just as easily.

Jenni asked me, in those last few days, how I could have been so sure, so absolutely positive that this was how it would all work out. Do you know what I told her? I told her that he loves easily. Logan Drake doesn't make you *earn* his love, if he loves you, he loves you. What you *do* earn is his continued love, respect and trust. The man is loyal, sometimes to a fault and I knew Jenni could see it. They were so similar it made me laugh when they argued but I saw in my last weeks that they managed to get over it, mostly and I'm glad.

Unfortunately, I won't be around to see how they behave into the future but I know they both want what's best for you and therefore, they'll do what they can to get along.

I wish I could be there to see you grow, to get older, to experience life but I won't and whether we think that's fair or not, it is the way it is.

What I want for you is love. I want you to feel loved and to love freely. Don't hold onto the pain of losing your mum too early to this horrible disease. I don't want you to hate. To hate cancer, to hate anyone who has both parents or their mums. You got a shitty deal, we both did but you got a dad and a step-dad in return.

I want you to enjoy life. To make the most of every chance and opportunity you get. Not to say that you have to do everything that you're presented with, you're allowed to say no and be free to say it. Say it often and say it loud. You don't have to do things that you don't want to (except school and what your dad and Julian tell you to), anything else, any opportunity that you get the chance at and you want to do it, grab it by both hands and take your best shot baby girl and know that I will be watching you, helping you as much as I can.

And know that in the end, I had no choice *but* to believe that it would work. I was dying and you needed a family and Logan is that family. I know without a doubt that your Dad loves you unconditionally.

I love you, Savannah Rae Drake. I will always love you. Nothing, no distance, even death, can ever change that.

Mum xoxox

Part .2.

Savannah

The first time my dad gave me a letter on my birthday, I was ten. I didn't know at the time that I would get one on every birthday.

Opening that envelope and recognising my Mum's handwriting brought tears to my eyes. I was grateful that my dad knew I would be feeling emotional and he gave me that letter while I was in my bedroom, alone and left me to read it, while also making it clear, that he would be waiting for me if I needed to talk or just cuddle.

Opening one every year on my birthday was the one gift I looked forward to every year. Dad and Papa knew that anything they gave to me for my birthday would be well received and I would love them and it but that letter? That letter meant everything to me.

The memories and history that I hadn't thought about in forever, always made me smile through the tears. I miss her so much, that need to talk to her never goes away but I know she's happy for me now. She always told me about Logan Drake, I always knew who my father was. Logan and his existence was never a secret, much to Aunt Jenni's confusion. She never could understand why mum was so eager to talk about him and tell me about their time together.

I can't helping laughing every time I see them together now and I wonder if somehow mum knows. Does she know that her best friend and ex-boyfriend are now the best of friends? Even if they do still behave like they don't like each other!

Today, is my 18th birthday. I don't know if this is the last letter from my Mum and I can't bring myself to open it and read it. Instead, I open up the bright yellow filing box that has all the mementos and letters from previous years.

DARLING SAVANNAH,

By now you've been with your dad and Julian for a year or so and I know, without a doubt, that life is amazing for the three of you. I also know, without a doubt, that you have a circle of people around you that love you unconditionally. They're not your new family, they're simply your family. They've always been there, we just haven't always been with them.

I know things have been tough and I know you miss me but I want you to know that I'm proud of you, I'll always be proud of you.

Live life. Be happy. Be proud and most of all, be kind.

Love Mum xoxox

It was short but it was sweet and it also contained a birthday card that she must have gotten somewhere between grandma's house and the cottage.

I have no idea how or when she managed to buy cards and paper to write these letters and set up all the cards and letters for all the years that I received them but I have no doubt Aunt Jenni had a lot to do with them, as did my Dad, Papa and Aunt Kenna.

Every year was a similar letter.

Darling Savannah,

You're now 13 and undoubtedly it's a time you need your mum around to talk about things. I hope that Aunt Jenni is still with you to help you through everything. We had many discussions about how I would have approached things if I was still with you and so, I hope that Aunt Makenna is helping you as well. I'm not sure how much help Dad or Julian will be but I know that they'll both try.

I hope you're happy. I know you're safe, well loved and cared for but I hope that you're happy. That's what matters in this crazy thing we call life and that's what I want the most for you. Happiness.

Happiness, joy and absolute love. I will always be proud of you.

Live life. Be happy. Be proud and most of all, be kind.

Love Mum xoxox

Another short but sweet note. Dad can't tell me when Mum wrote these letters. Either he doesn't know or he doesn't want to tell me but I get the feeling that she wrote them in the those few weeks we lived in the cottage before she died. They're so short, to the point and she knew who she was leaving me with.

She's not wrong though, Aunt Jenni and Aunt Kenna helped me through puberty in a way that Dad and Papa just couldn't. They tried, god love them but they just they couldn't understand everything that was happening. They never hesitated in buying my supplies, pads, tampons, whatever I needed but they just couldn't understand the changes I was going through. Or the emotions that suddenly hit me as well.

Aunt Jenni lived in the cottage much more in my teenage years. I didn't recognise that at the time but as I sit here, looking back and wondering what our life would have looked like if my Mum was still here, I realise that she made sacrifices for me.

I'm sitting on the back porch, watching Jaspa, the gorgeous golden retriever that my dad's got me eight years ago. I can hear the family, my dads, my uncles, my aunts and of course, Grams Susan and Gramps Harold, all doing things and making things inside the house. Normally, I would be in there helping them, it *is* for my birthday after all but today, is different. Today is harder than all the other birthdays that my Mum has missed in the last decade. It's a big one and even though I know there will be bigger days ahead that she will miss, my 21st birthday, my wedding day, the birth of my first child and so many others in between. This one feels like the first *big* milestone that she's missing.

I open the letter that my dad gave me on my 16th birthday, the last big birthday I guess. I'm not sure what I'm looking for and definitely don't know if I'll find it but I know I need to read it. It won't be the second time I've read it, I've read all of these letters probably a hundred times over.

This one, however, is a little wrinkled. You could assume that it would be because I've read it so many times but in all honestly, it's from the tears that fall every time I read it.

Sweet 16

Darling Savannah,

Wow! Sixteen! This is a big one and I can't quite believe you've made it. Unfortunately, you made it without me. As you know by now, I left these letters with your dad, each one had a wrapped gift with them. Some I got myself along the way once I knew I had weeks with you. Some of those gifts your step-dad helped me find when we moved into the cottage.

This year, I need you to talk to your Aunt Jenni.

When I first found out I was sick and the treatment wasn't working, Jenni and I planned. We planned for your the future where perhaps I might not be around. She didn't like it, for obvious reasons but she let me do what I needed to do at the time.

I know your dad gave you a gift from me already and this isn't about that gift not being enough or me keeping anything from him, it's more about something that Jenni and I shared. Something that she will want to give herself.

Happy sweet 16 my beautiful girl.

I hope that your life is full of happiness, joy and absolute love. I will always be proud of you.

Live life. Be happy. Be proud and most of all, be kind.

Love Mum xoxox

I knew that Aunt Jenni was in the cottage, she'd gotten in the night before my birthday and sent me a message to say she was here. My dads had given me a phone for my birthday a day early and when my first message was Aunt Jenni, I knew why I'd been given it early.

Dad gave me the letter and gift, then left me in peace. This had become our routine every year since that first time and I appreciated having a few minutes to myself to be with my mum in this way before there was a big family get to-gether where they all fussed over me and made me feel more loved than any kid should feel. I'd never once felt like they were doing it to *make* me feel welcomed into the family, it was just how they were and I was welcomed because Logan Drake was my father.

I opened the back door to ask if it was OK if I went over to see Aunt Jenni but Papa beat me to it.

"Your Aunt Jenni is waiting for you Sweetheart. Leila dropped breakfast over there a few minutes ago, so you should get over there while it's still hot." He came over, dropped a quick kiss to the top off my head and then left me to it.

"Go have some time with Jenni, Savannah. Take as long as you need, we'll be here whenever you get back." My dad told me as he took me into his arms. Let me tell you something about my dad, he gives the best bear hugs on the planet and I loved them. Even as a teenager, I found a way to get one from him. I'm not ashamed to admit, that I've played on their fear of having a teenager in the house and turned on the waterworks for one of those hugs. The thing is, I know I don't have to do anything except *ask* for a hug but making him think that he's helping me at the same time is a real bonus to me. He also squeezes tightly and I always feel safe and secure in his arms.

I didn't need to knock on the cottage door, it was open, waiting for me to enter.

"Good morning, Sav. Happy 16th birthday darling girl." I closed the door behind me and when I turn back to the open living area of the cottage, I'm engulfed in another warm hug.

"Thanks Aunt Jenni." I smile, pulling out of her hug.

"Did Dad give you your letter?" She asked, leading me over the small table that we've shared countless meals at. "Is that why you're here?"

"He did and yes, it's why I'm here but I would have come over this morning anyway, you know that." I smile as she poured herself a coffee and a hot chocolate for me.

"I know, I guess I was just checking to see if you'd read your Mum's letter.

"I'm not here *just* to see what you have for me." I muttered, even though we're both very much aware that I'm here because I want to know what they chose for me.

"Eat something." She points at all the food on the table that I know, without a doubt is going to be delicious but I don't really want any right now. Aunt Jenni seems to sense that and laughed as she pulled out small gift box from somewhere. "Here. Happy sweet 16 sweet girl. Your mum and I found this and she wanted you to have it today. Not a day sooner, not a birthday any sooner, which is why it wasn't put with all the others."

"Because it's from the both of you?" I asked, curious.

"That too." She'd smiled. "Open it." I didn't feel like opening it front of her. I'd never opened any gifts from Mum in front of others before but I understood why I had to this time.

Without saying a word, I take the gift from her hand without saying a word. I'm not sure what to say and I'm not sure I can speak right now. The anticipation of what this might be is insane and my sixteen year old brain just couldn't think.

The silence in the cottage is almost a living being, at least back then in my overly dramatic teenage brain that's how it felt. The only sound was ripping paper and my breathing, which seemed ridiculously loud to me.

"Oh my -." I stopped myself from saying more because I knew that she didn't like any kind of cursing coming out of my mouth. "When did you two do this?" I asked, my voice barely above a whisper. Fingers are clasped around the red velvet box and I can feel the tears welling.

"We saw you looking at it a few times over time and decided to get it but when we went back they didn't have any left." Aunt Jenni explained with a smile. "Then online shopping exploded so I went in search of it. I found it just before your Mum was diagnosed. I ordered it but then, well you know what happened. When it arrived, she wanted me to give it to you today. I tried to convince her over time and even more so when we moved in here, to give to you herself but she refused. She was steadfast that she wanted you to have it today."

My 18th birthday

As I sit here, on the back porch of our home listening to the others inside setting up the celebrations, my hand reaches up to the chain hanging from my neck. Dad bought a new chain for it last year because it broke but the rest is the same.

A delicate gold filagree butterfly, with four gemstones in it. The three birthstones of the three women who mean more to me than I could ever express and mine, all connected forever despite that half of us are no longer here anymore.

"Hey." I jump at that single word as my Uncle Caleb sits down beside me on the step. "How ya doin' kiddo?" He asks as he bumps my shoulder with his. My mum wasn't wrong, Uncle Caleb has been the fun uncle for as long as I've known him but he's also one of the most caring men I know. Uncle Brady might be the more serious of the two of them but he's just as much fun in his own special way. I love them both beyond belief.

All of the men in my life are caring and not afraid to show any kind of love or affection to anyone that they care about. It's helped me to know exactly what I want in my own life because men like this bunch are hard to find. This family, *my* family are loud, loving and in my business but they love me unconditionally.

"Yeah, I'm OK." I tell him, bumping my shoulder back into his but not looking up to meet his eyes.

"Are you going to read that letter?"

"I don't know." I answer quietly.

"What's stopping you this year kiddo?" He asks, his voice not *as* quiet as mine but subdued none the less. I didn't know he had it in him to be that quiet. "You're usually waiting to read them every year, what's different this year?" He doesn't push me to answer, he lets me sit and think about it for a few minutes. I don't feel pressure to tell him anything, I *do* feel the desire to explain it to someone other than myself. To get it off my chest and hopefully move on with the rest of my day.

"I feel it more today, I guess." I say, still not looking up. "I feel it more today that she's not here than I have any other birthday previously. This one is more significant. This one makes me an adult. This one just seems to be making me miss her more than before."

"You're allowed to miss your mum, Savvy. No-one is ever going to judge you for that. Your Dad won't be upset *because* you're missing her, only that he can't help you feel better. You know that, right? Both of them would do anything they could to make this better for you. We all would."

"Yeah, I know but these feelings aren't anything you guys can do anything about. I don't feel alone or lost *because* I have all of you. The entire family loved me without even thinking about it. You took Mum and Jenni in too and I know they appreciated it, even if it took Jenni some time to show it." We both laugh and it feels good.

"We wouldn't have had it any other way, I hope you know that Savvy. Nothing about you living here was *ever* a hardship or even something that we considered not doing. Your dads certainly didn't hesitate for a second and the rest, we didn't just fall in line Savvy, we wanted you guys here. You *have* to know that. From the minute your dad found out about you, he wanted to know you. Your mum being sick certainly made that happen sooner than what might have been considered 'normal' but let's face it, this family isn't what most people would consider normal anyway." I can't help laughing at his assessment.

"Everyone has been welcoming and I mean that you've all embraced us without a second thought. You're right though, I've never felt anything other than loved by everyone around us, that's not something I've ever even thought about. Even when I was teased at school for having two dads, I didn't care." I take a deep breath. "It's just this birthday seems more than the rest. I've finished high school, I'm an adult and making adult choices. I guess, I'm understanding why she made certain choices and would love to have a conversation with her. I just miss her."

"I know." It's a simple statement and I know he understands how I feel, he lost both of his parents around the age I am now. We sit there in silence for a few minutes and it's comfortable. "I'm going to go back inside and see if Leila needs a hand with anything. You know she won't ask and probably won't take the offer off anyone else." He winks and leaves me alone.

I unwrap the gift and open another velvet box to discover a gold guardian angel charm nestled in a bed of soft white silk, that glitters in the sunlight. It's beautiful.

Darling Savannah,

This is a big deal birthday and I wish I was able to be there with you. Your 18th birthday is a right of passage and your official step into becoming an adult. You have no idea how much I wish I was there with you but I know that you're surrounded with people who love you more than even you can imagine.

I want you to know that I am with you always. I am helping you with every decision and every step that you take, I will be guiding you in your life. I may not physically be by your side, I am still with you.

Aunt Jenni went out and found exactly what I wanted to give you today so that you would know that I would always be with you. I want you to carry it with you always and know that I am with you.

Happy 18th birthday, my beautiful girl.

I hope that your life is full of happiness, joy and absolute love. I will always be proud of you.

Live life. Be happy. Be proud and most of all, be kind.

Love Mum xoxox

I love that she signs off her letters in exactly the same way every year. It's very much like her and it makes me feel like she's here.

I look at the small gift sitting beside me, wrapped in paper with butterflies, in beautiful colours and I'm assuming it might just match the necklace my fingers can't stop touching. It's my physical connection to my mum. I look back, over my shoulder to check on everyone else and all I see is my family, happy, smiling and getting shit done. None of them are watching me, wondering what I'm doing or thinking, or if I'm OK and that relaxes me enough to pick up the gift and unwrap it.

When I open the small velvet box, another very small note falls out and my mum's handwriting is on it: *Savannah, let this be your guide through life. I love you xx*

Inside, is a gold angel charm. I run my thumb over the surface because it's glittering in the sun and I want to know how it feels.

"They're chips of diamonds." I jump when Aunt Jenni speaks behind me. "Sorry, I didn't mean to startle you. I know you like to have your alone time with these gifts but I wanted to explain this one."

"What's to explain?" I'm confused because she's felt the need to explain any of the others, not on purpose anyway.

"Can I put it on your necklace?"

"Sure." I wasn't sure where I was going to put it but that makes sense I suppose. I turn my back to her and she opens the clasp, slips the angel on there and closes it again in silence.

"Now, you're protected." She says smiling as I turn back to look at her.

"I'm always protected, Aunt Jenni." I'm still confused, I have no idea what's going on.

"I know." She says, looking back towards the house filled with family. "But this one is your mum, always with you."

"I don't need a charm to have her with me." I feel defensive, like she's accusing me of forgetting my mum and not thinking about her just because I have Dad and Papa, plus the rest of the gang. "She's always with me in my heart."

"I know darling but this way, *she* can be with you." She smiles and heads back inside and I feel like I missed something in her explanation but I don't have the time to think about it because my friends have started to arrive, which means the party is starting.

My 21st birthday

This year, I'm away at university and my dad told me that I didn't have to come home if I didn't want to but I wake up on my 21st birthday in the cottage because that's where I wanted to be. I haven't spent a birthday away from Drake Wines in over a decade and I don't see that changing any time soon.

I can hear Aunt Jenni moving around the cottage and I wonder if she's setting up the breakfast that I have no doubt Leila sent over this morning. We can cook in the cottage but we rarely have to thanks to Leila and her talented staff at Vines.

I look over to the drawers next to my bed to look at either the clock or to pick up my phone and instead find a beautifully wrapped gift sitting there. I have no freaking idea when Jenni managed to sneak in here because I'm generally a pretty light sleeper and hear all kinds of movement but we had a few drinks last night, so that might have helped her sneakiness.

I reach out and bring the gift over to my chest. This time it has curly ribbon wrapped around it and I have to laugh because I can't believe that Aunt Jenni did *this*. I mean, she's not a bells and whistles, frills kind of woman, so I have a feeling that my stepdad had something to do with this one because every gift I've ever received from him and my dad has had something extra on it, bows, ribbons, you name it!

An envelope drops quietly to the bed next to me when I pick up the gift and I decide to open the gift first, for the first time ever because I'm just not ready to read what my mum might have to say to me on my twenty first birthday. I thought I missed her on my eighteenth birthday, today my heart is a kind of sore that just aches like it might break because I've met the man I want to marry while at university and he will never get to meet my mum. That being said though, he *has* gotten to meet my dad, my stepdad, Aunt Jenni and the rest of the Drakes and they've *all* embraced him with all of their hearts. That makes me happier than I could ever explain to them.

I unwrap the gift, open yet another velvet gift box and I can't help laughing. Every gift left by my mum for an 'important' birthday has been in one of those weird, red velvet gift boxes. The familiarity but old fashioned tradition makes me both laugh and cry. When I open the box the tears stream freely down my face.

Inside is a delicate, beautiful gold bracelet that matches the butterfly necklace that she left for me five years ago. Only this time instead of the birthstones of all the women that mean the world to me, there are two stones set into the wings of the butterfly and they're my dad and stepdads. I know this because Papa and I have discussed *everyone's* birthstones on multiple occasions. The fact that my mum and Jenni knew that this would mean the world to me *and* what their birthstones *are* make it even more special to me.

Taking a deep breath, I reach for the letter with my name on it in my mum's handwriting and I feel a fresh batch of tears fall. In the background I can hear Aunt Jenni pottering around in the main part of the cottage but in here, all I can hear is my own breathing. Steeling myself I open the envelope, take out the paper and unfold it.

This part of every birthday doesn't get easier. It doesn't feel great, even though I know *why* she did this and I appreciate the effort, sometimes I wish she hadn't because it makes it fresh every damned year. My birthday comes with an almost foreboding feeling every year.

My darling Savannah,

This year is your 21st and I wish I was there with you to see the woman you've become but, obviously I'm not. I know that you're an amazing woman. I know without a doubt that I would be, I am, proud of you. Beyond proud because I know that you're surrounded by the most amazing human beings that you could be but that doesn't mean I don't wish that I was there with you today.

As I sit here, writing this letter, I can't help wondering what you look like today. All I know is the young girl you were and I wish I could see you now. I can imagine how you might look, dark hair, past your shoulders, in loose curls, brown eyes sparkling with excitement at your birthday like they always did when you were a little girl.

I find myself wondering if you've found someone to love and I hope that they love you without reservation and I hope that you love them back in the same way. I know that Logan and Julian will have shown you how to love and to accept love, I just hope that my death hasn't given you any reason to not want to share your life with someone for fear of losing them.

Life and death are the only two guarantees in life Savannah Rae (well and taxes!) but you can't stop either from happening. One pretty much leads to the other.

I hope that Jenni is still in your life and that she's shown you the love of a mother in my absence. I know that you have Makenna in your life now as well but Jenni has been with you, us, since the beginning and she loves you as if you were her own.

I hope that your life is full of happiness, joy and absolute love. I will always be proud of you.

Happy 21ˢᵗ birthday my darling girl.
Live life. Be happy. Be proud and most of all, be kind.
Love Mum xoxox

It's the longest letter I've had in a few years and I'm struggling to breathe through my tears. I'm not sure how long I've been sitting there, the letter clutched to my chest with one hand and the bracelet clasped tightly in my other hand, when there's a light tap on the bedroom door.

"Come in." I croak out around my tears.

"Good morning beautiful girl. How are you doing?" Aunt Jenni asks as she sits on the edge of the bed.

"I'm peachy." I smile through the tears that are still damp on my cheeks.

"Oh Honey." She rubs my leg through the covers. "I can't help wondering if these letters are a good thing or not. I know they helped you when you were young and we'd just lost Lori but I've wondered for a few years now whether they do more harm than good." Her smile is sad and I feel the need to reassure her but I can't.

"I've come to dread my birthday to be honest." I drop my eyes to my hands that are resting on my stomach, still holding the letter and the bracelet. I'm embarrassed and kind of ashamed of admitting to feeling that way. "Don't get me wrong, I appreciate the effort, yours and hers but it's just that I know I'm getting one and I know it's going to make me miss her. It's not like I don't miss her every other day of the year but I think that perhaps the letters are too much now. I love the gifts and I appreciate that you've made the effort with them all these years."

"It has never been a chore, Savannah." She smiles at me. "But I never meant for them to make you not look forward to your birthday."

"It's just that I know they're coming and I'm going to have to deal with them first thing." Before she can speak, I rush on. "I miss her, every day Jenni, but the thing is, this is my birthday. I want to celebrate, I want to be happy. I feel like a complete arsehole for saying it but I feel even worse for saying it out loud. I know that this was her plan, that she wanted me to read them on my birthday, Dad explained it to me back with the first letter. At the beginning, I enjoyed them and couldn't wait for the next one but they've become a sad reminder that she's not here. That she can't celebrate with me, with *us*. That she'll never meet Lucas and get to know him. I won't get her opinion on him and whether she thinks I'm doing the right thing or not. She'll miss my wedding, my kids. All of it. And these letters? These letters just ram that home to me every year and every year it gets worse. I come home because I don't want to do it at school because I know *one* of you will bring it with you anyway and I don't want to take it *there*. That's where I'm not the little girl who lost her Mum to cancer too young. There is where people aren't sad *for* me, they're sad *with* me if I happen to be sad but mostly, I'm just Savannah Drake. I'm known for who and how I am *there*, not where I've come from."

I didn't realise that I gotten so worked up and emotional as I spoke until I'd finished and I was gulping for air and the covers were damp from the tears that I didn't hold back for the first time in years. The guilt I feel this morning, is stronger than I've been feeling for years because I've finally voiced how I'm feeling.

"When did you start not looking forward to them?" Her voice is soft and I know she's trying not to judge me but I can't help feeling really defensive.

"It doesn't matter. Forget I said anything." I start to move off the bed so that I can go have a shower and cry in peace. "I have to get moving anyway, Lucas will be here soon."

"Savannah Rae Drake, you sit your arse down right now!" Her voice is stern, almost angry. I can't recall *ever* having it directed at *me* and it stops me in my tracks. "You don't get to drop all of that and walk away, Savannah."

"I don't want to talk about it." It's simple because I don't. I've already said more than I ever thought I would.

"Well, that's too bad because you've started now and I'm going to finish it." I don't look at her, I can't. "Sit down and get comfy, Lucas can and *will* wait." She waits until I've settled back down on the bed before she starts speaking again. "*When* did these letters stop becoming something to look forward to for you?" I take my time to think before answering her. It's got more to do with finding the right words to express what I want to say.

"When I turned sixteen." I mutter.

"Speak up, Savannah, you're not a child darling, you're an adult. An adult who has gone through more in her life than most of us have to deal with in our lives but that doesn't mean that you get a pass with this. You're stronger than that!" I can feel her disappointment and it hurts. I haven't had this conversation with Dad or Papa.

"On my sixteenth birthday." I say louder, not quite stronger but definitely louder. "When I sat on the steps in the backyard and stared at the gift that I knew I would open *after* reading the letter."

"Is it the gifts or the letters?" She asks, nodding her head thoughtfully.

"The letters. I appreciate the gifts more than you can imagine and I feel like that makes me materialistic and that it would disappoint Mum, my Dads, you and everyone else around me." I sigh. "But that's not why I like the gifts. I *love* the gifts because they give something real, something tangible to hold on to and remember her with. That she chose it, if not *that* one specifically, she had the idea of what she wanted me to have to remind me that my mother is still a part of my life."

"So, the letters are too much?" She looks confused and I know she's trying to understand.

"Sort of." I close my eyes and take a deep breath before opening them again and meeting my aunts. "I don't hate them, I love those letters. The short ones, the long ones and everything in between, I just don't like being given them on my birthday anymore. It was amazing and comforting in the beginning. That first one was exactly what I needed, as were the ones that followed but by the time I was sixteen, it wasn't something that I looked forward to. Not for my birthday, anyway."

"Have you told Logan or Jules about how you feel?" There's a small amount of hurt in the tone of her voice as she expects me to say yes but I shake my head.

"No, I haven't told anyone."

"Well now, I think we both know that's not true, don't we Savannah?" I don't know *how* she knows but she's right, it's the reason that Lucas is coming here first thing this morning. He couldn't make it last night but he did leave first thing to get here, hoping that he could get here before this hit me. He didn't.

I'm saved from answering when voices and loud noises come from the front of the cottage.

"Speak of the devil." I smile widely, causing my amazing aunt to shake her head but she's smiling as she does it.

"I'm glad he's here for you Savannah. You deserve some happiness in your life."

"Of course she does!" My dad's voice says from the doorway. "Lucas is here. We saw his car from Vines, so we decided to follow him up here to see you this morning." His smile is so bright and so loving, it makes me feel even worse about what I just confessed to Aunt Jenni and I burst into a fresh round of tears. I barely notice as Jenni gets up from the end of the bed where she was sitting and talks quietly to my dad, then leaves us alone, closing the door behind her.

"Ohhh Sweetheart! I wish you'd told me sooner that the letters were upsetting you." He says, pulling me in close and I'm engulfed in his arms, which is one of my favourite places to be. He gives the biggest and *best* bear hugs in existence. As much as I love Lucas and being held by him, nothing quite beats being held in this bear hug from my Dad.

"I. Didn't. Know. How." I sob. "I didn't. Want you. To. Be. Maaaaad." I force it between the sobs wracking my body, the last word coming out as a whine like I'm nine years old again!

"Oh Sweetheart! We got through the teenage years with very little trauma to us all but I *do* wish you'd spoken to me about *this*. These letters were never meant to upset or hurt you, they were meant to give you some peace and guidance. I think we all know how much you miss your Mum, I mean, in a weird way I miss her as well. I wish that I'd gotten to know her as an adult and as your mum but we didn't get the chance and that makes me sad."

"I'm sorry the teenage years weren't as easy as they could have been." I choke out between catching my breath and a few small sobs.

"They weren't anywhere near as bad as they could have been, Sweetheart. You weren't around when Uncle Caleb was a teenager, trust me, it could have been *so* much worse." I can't help laughing because I can imagine my uncle making life difficult for everyone around when he was in his teen years and I know that's why my dad said it, to make me laugh. "Honestly, I wish I'd known because I wouldn't have given them to you on your birthday if I'd known they were making you sad I would have worked out another time for you to receive them. What I'm saying, Savannah is that we could have worked this all out and I'm disappointed that you didn't feel like you could talk to at least *one* of us about it, if not me, before this. I never want to see you so sad and upset, Sweetheart."

"I didn't want to upset anyone because I knew everyone else was dealing with their own feelings of loss." I shrug my shoulders, trying to pass my feelings off as not that important but he won't have it.

"Nothing is more important than you, Savannah." I raise an eyebrow at him and he laughs. "You're right, I hope Jules didn't hear me say that!"

"Look, it's not a big deal. Not really." I reassure him because he raises his eyebrow at me now. "I just feel overly sensitive about it all today and -"

"And what?"

"And I feel selfish, OK? I'm not the only kid who has lost a parent. Plus, I have you and Papa, not to mention everyone else we have around us. I've been lucky."

"That doesn't mean you don't miss your *mum,* Savannah." He pulls me back into his chest, I'd managed to pull out of it so that I could talk but he draws me back in and it feels so fucking good that I can't make myself pull away again. "We love you more than you know but if you ever keep something like this from us again, just know that you'll never be too old for me to whoop your butt!"

"I love you, Dad."

"I love you too, Savannah."

"Can anyone get in on this lovefest?" Papa's voice asks but I can't see him because I'm still squished against my Dad's chest.

"Of course! All are welcome!" There's a loud chorus of whooping and then the bed is covered in people and my sad mood is gone because I am surrounded by love.

"I love you too, Savannah." Papa says quietly in my ear.

"I love you more." Uncle Caleb says louder.

"Oh no you don't! I love her so much, I'm going to marry her." The whole room stops at Lucas' declaration and people part so that I can see him.

He's kneeling beside the bed, a ring box open as he asks, "Will you marry me Savannah Bishop Drake? Will you give me the greatest joy and be my wife?" I look at my Dad, then Papa and they're both smiling through their tears, nodding. Then I look at Aunt Jenni and she looks the same. When I look back at Lucas, he looks nervous and I realise I've left him hanging.

"Yes." My voice is barely above a whisper, so I cough and says louder, stronger. "Yes! Yes Lucas Deans, I will absolutely make you my husband."

"Yeah?" He asks.

"Don't ask her again man, you already did that, put the ring on her finger before she changes her mind!" Uncle Caleb jokes but it seems to be enough to jolt Lucas out of his stunned stillness because he jumps up and pushes the ring onto my finger and pulls me into a tight hug. It's not quite a bear hug the likes of which I get off my Dad but that's OK, it's a safe space anyway.

"I wanted to make today a happier day for you. I love you, Savannah Bishop Drake , soon to be Deans." He whispers in my ear.

"I love you more, Lucas Deans." I whisper back.

"Time to party!" Uncle Caleb yells and everyone filters out of the room.

"Congratulations! We love you both and we're just so happy for you." Dad says, his arm around Papa's shoulders, who has his arm wrapped tightly around his husband's waist. They've both got tears in their eyes.

"Thank you." We start to follow the others out to living area but I stop and so do they. "Hang on, you don't seem surprised. Did you two know about this?" I ask my Dad's, who both chuckle.

"Yeah, they did. I asked them both if they would be happy to welcome me into the family." Lucas answers for them.

"And *we* were more than happy to say yes. I mean he's already family anyway, why not make it official, right?" My Dad, the man who intimidated every boyfriend I had as a teen says with a huge smile and *that's* how I know he loves Lucas.

"Let's go join the party before Caleb does something that we'll all regret." Papa says and we all laugh.

"I need to have a shower and get changed!" I say suddenly realising I'm still in my pyjama's.

"It can wait until after breakfast. You look beautiful anyway." Lucas says. "Let's not give the family a chance to organise a wedding without our input, OK?"

He has a point, so I let him lead me into the living area where all the people I love and who love me are gathered.

I send up a silent thank you to Mum for bringing this crazy family *and* Lucas to me because I know she had a hand in it. I wish she was here but she can't be and that's OK, too.

The night before my wedding

Today is the night before my wedding and while traditionally brides and grooms to be, have their bachelorette and bachelor parties tonight, Lucas and I had ours weeks ago. Neither of us wanted to show up tomorrow hungover or hurt. Instead, we're in separate cottages at Drake Wines.

To be honest, I barely left before I returned. I went to university and studied business, just like my Dad. Funnily enough, Lucas is an accountant, like my Papa. I guess there's something to be said for looking for men like our fathers!

Speaking of my dad's, they wanted me to stay at the house but I wanted some space. So, I'm staying in the cottage that my Aunt Jenni lives at least part of the year in. We've had a few drinks with Kenna, Leila, Sara, Morgan, Kirsty and Maggie. The last three being my bridesmaids and already in bed. Leila went home well before then because she's doing the catering tomorrow and Kenna went home too because she wouldn't take no for an answer *and* she's the wedding planner!

Jenni starts telling me stories about her adventures with my mum when they were younger and I realise after the first couple, that she's had a bit to drink and I should probably help her to bed, when she says something that makes me stop and listen.

"You know, your mum and I got into so much trouble before she had you. Well to be fair, I got into trouble and Lori just always happened to be there right beside me." Jenni laughs. "She was my ride or die."

"Oh my god! You were in love with her, weren't you?" I ask, my hand stops halfway to my mouth with what I'd planned to be my last drink of the night but now I may need a drink to come to grips with the fact that I never noticed that Jenni's love went further than friendship. "That's why you dropped everything and helped us. It's also why you haven't been in a relationship, isn't it?"

"I've had relationships they've just never gone far." She smiles but it doesn't quite reach her eyes and I feel sad for her. Unrequited love is never a fun prospect no matter who you are or how old the love is.

"Did she know? Did my mum know?" I want to know but I don't want to find out that my mum kept my aunt around because she knew that she loved her.

"No." Jenni shakes her head. "Not until the end."

"You never told her before that?" I'm astonished that someone could not tell someone they're that close to that they love them or that someone that close to them could not know.

"I did but at the end."

"Why did you wait? How could she NOT know?"

"I think she did. At least that's the impression I got when I finally confessed the truth to her." This time her smile is filled with sadness.

"What did she say?"

"She said she loved me too." Jenni stares at the wall, I think she's remembering, I could almost believe she doesn't even know I'm here anymore. "I told her that wasn't what I meant, that I didn't love her like a friend, that I was in love with her. She agreed, said she understood but not sure she did. It was right near the end there, I'm not sure if you remember what she was like, you were pretty young and we tried to shelter you from the very worst of it. I don't know if she was just mumbling into the unknown or if she was talking to me. All I know for sure is that I got it off my chest and I know she understood me, I just don't know if she meant she loved me, like I loved her. Either way, she was gone not much long after."

"Is that why you've been around all these years? Because of your love for my mum?" I feel like that needy, scared little girl I was back when mum first died.

"You think I stayed here and helped your dads with you over the years for some weird connection you might give me to Lori? No." She shakes her head so aggressively that I'm worried about her doing some damage. "No, I've stayed because I wanted to and yes, I did promise Lori that I would always be here for you but it was where I wanted to be. I knew that Logan and Jules would give you everything you needed and the rest of their families would welcome you, love you without reservations. Were you a connection to Lori? Sure I guess but I love you because of you Savannah, never doubt that."

"I love you too, Jenni. Now, I think it's time we got you into a bed, I need you bright and happy tomorrow morning, not hungover and sad." I take her glass from her hand and place both hers and mine on the sink, I'll get to them in the morning. "Come on, let's get you to bed."

She doesn't argue and I'm grateful because I don't think I could handle her if she did. When we make it to her room, I lie her down on her bed and pull the covers over her. We'd all put our pyjamas on to get comfortable earlier so that made my life easier.

"Goodnight sweet Savannah. Lori would be so proud of the woman you've become. I love you like the daughter I never had." I feel the tears welling in my eyes.

"Goodnight Jenni, I love you too." She hums and then she's quietly snoring. I make my way to my bedroom and sit on the edge of the bed. I pull out my phone to message my dad.

Me: *did you know Jenni was in love with my mum?*

Dad: *I never knew for sure but I thought it was likely. Why?*

Me: *she just confessed to me*

Dad: *oh wow! How do you feel about that and how much did she drink?*

Me: *She drank a little bit*

Dad: *How do you feel about it?*

Me: *Sad.*

Me: *Sad that mum let Jenni help us if she knew and sad if mum didn't know and Jenni didn't confess until it was too late.*

Dad: *she confessed to your mum?*

Me: *just before she died apparently*

Dad: *This is not your issue, Savannah. They were adults, their friendship was what it was. Their love whether romantic or platonic had nothing to do with you or their love for you*

He's not wrong about that but I still feel bad for Jenni.

Me: *I know you're right. I love you Dad and Papa. See you both in the morning.*

Dad: *We love you too darling girl. See you in the morning xx*

I can't help laughing because I know that if Papa isn't reading the messages as well, dad would be reading them out to him. I send one last message and then get myself into bed.

Me: See you in the morning Lucas. I love you
Lucas: I love you more and I can't wait to be your husband xxxxx

I smile at the phone and know that the morning will bring me a happiness that I never thought I would find.

My wedding day

Today is bittersweet. On the one hand, it's the happiest day of my life! I'm marrying the man of my dreams, the one I plan on spending the rest of my life with. On the other hand, I have the reminder that life doesn't always go the way you planned because my Mum isn't here to share my day.

"Hey, are you OK?" Kirsty, my maid of honour asks quietly, her hand resting on my upper arm.

"Yeah, I'm OK." I tell her, smiling because I honestly can say I *am* OK.

"Today can't be easy for you, so if you need some space, just let me know and I'll get this rowdy bunch to shut up and give you some peace." She says, aiming her thumb over her shoulder in the direction of the bridesmaids and my Aunts sharing a bottle of champagne and laughing.

"They're good, Kirsty." I hug her tight with one arm. "Trust me when I say, being around this crazy bunch makes me happier than you can imagine." We both laugh and get pulled into the fray of bubbles and more loud laughter.

We all take turns in the make-up chair and then the hairdresser's chair but, while the girls get their dresses on after all of that is done, I stay in the white silk robe that Kenna gave me early this morning.

"Before I kick you all out so that I can get into my dress, I want to say something." I say loudly to grab their attention and wait for them all to quieten down. "I want to thank you ladies, all of you, for being here with me but not just for today. Each and every one of you have influenced my life in positive ways and I love you all. Jenni is the link to my Mum and I know how much they loved each other." I raise my glass in her direction and watch as a light blush creeps up her cheeks. She definitely remembers her confession last night and now I feel bad, because it wasn't my intention to embarrass her. "Kenna and Leila have taught me *so* many different things here at Drake Wines that I find their knowledge, expertise and unconditional love things that I know I would struggle without." I raise my glass in their direction and they yell out.

"We love you more!" Then collapse into giggles and I make a note to remove the bubbles from them before they get too much further along in their celebrations.

"And to the three best friends I could ever ask for. Morgan, Kirsty and Maggie. What would I have done without you three when I first arrived here? I would have been lost and I love the three of you more than you'll ever know."

"We love you too." They chime in together giggling and I make another note to myself to take the bubbles away from everyone after this! "All of you are amazing, strong, independent and loving women and I don't know what I would do without any of you."

Suddenly, I'm surrounded by the six most amazing women I know, arms tangling together, trying to pull everyone into the same hug and I can't help laughing. This is why I love these women. There is no competition, they love and accept each other in ways that I admire.

"Alright, go out there and make sure everything is ready to go and let me get my dress on." I say. "Before we mess up our makeup and hair." They all laugh once again, flutes of bubbles left on the one table in the room, as they all file out the door without an argument. Jenni is the only one to stay behind.

"I'm sorry about last night." She starts, almost as soon as the door is shut behind Leila. "I shouldn't."

"I'm going to stop you right there. *You* have nothing to apologise for. I'm sorry that you were stuck in an unrequited love situation for so long but I know that she loved you in her own way. I don't know how deep that love went, if I'm being honest but know that she loved you."

"Oh, I know that. I just meant that I shouldn't have dumped all of that on you, any time but especially the night before your wedding. It was wrong."

"I'll admit the timing is something but that doesn't make the confession any less than the right thing to do. I'm glad you finally told me because I always wondered why you gave up so much to be with us. Now, I understand it. And before you say anything, I know you stayed in my life after her death because you love *me* like a daughter yourself, so you know, I'm not questioning that at all." I pull her into a hug. "I just wish you'd had more time with her and that you told her sooner."

"I'm grateful for the time that I *did* get to spend with her, especially at the end. I know that might sound strange but it was a privilege to hold her when she took her last breath." We stand there, arms wrapped tight around each other, for a minute, maybe two, before Jenni breaks out of the embrace and takes a step back. "Before we start getting too teary and you need your make-up touched up, let's stop this chat."

"OK, but it's only on hold. I want you to know that once we get home from Sandy Cove and visiting Samantha and Tomas, we *are* getting all of this out on the table." I warn her because I want to know everything.

"You've got a deal but today is your wedding day and that's all we're concentrating on." She steps over to her bag that's sitting on a couch and pulls out a small gift. "Now, I know you don't really want your card today because today is a happy occasion *but* I do have a gift for you. It's from all four of us."

I take the small package out of her hand and open the box. Unlike all the others, there's no wrapping paper and no velvet. This box has a pattern of wedding bells on it and it's beautiful.

"Oh my!" I gasp, my empty hand rising up to rest on my chest in shock. "This is beautiful."

"It's your something old and something blue. Your girls have something borrowed and something new for you." She smiles, taking the gorgeous hairclip out of the box . "Now, you don't have to wear it in your hair, you can clip it to your bouquet if you wish but we'd like you to carry it. Your Grandma left it to your Mum, hoping that she would be able to use it on *her* wedding day."

"Did Grammy wear it on her wedding day?"

"Yes, she did."

"I'm wearing it in my hair today."

Jenni helps me get into my form fitting, lacy wedding gown and then she goes out to call the hairdresser back in.

While I stand there waiting, there's a light knock on the door.

"You don't have to knock, Jenni."

"It's not Jenni. Can I come in?"

"Of course you can! You don't need to ask, Dad!"

"I didn't want to interrupt you girls." He says stepping into the room and closing the door behind him.

"The girls are all outside making sure things are ready to go." I tell him and I watch as he turns around and gets his first look at me.

"Oh my god, Savannah! You are *gorgeous*! I hope Lucas knows just how damned lucky he is and if he doesn't, well he'll have some questions to answer from a bunch of angry old men." He walks further into the room as he speaks but he hesitates when he reaches me. "Can I give you a hug? I don't want to wrinkle anything."

"Of course you can!" I laugh and then step into his open arms. I sigh as he wraps me up in that wonderful bear hug of his. "I love you, Dad."

"I love you more than you can ever imagine, Sweetheart."

"Are you ready for the hairdresser? Oh shit, sorry I didn't realise you were in here, Logan." Jenni says as she enters the room, without knocking I notice and I can't help laughing. I should have known better than to think she'd knock.

"That's OK, Jen, I'll get out of your hair and let you finished up. Call me when you're both ready to walk out there."

"No! Dad, stay. Please? We won't be long, right?" I look at the hairdresser, who smiles and shakes her head.

"We'll be a couple of minutes at the most, promise."

I take my Dad's hand in mine and plead with my eyes and he relaxes and stays with me.

"There. All done. You look absolutely gorgeous Savannah. Lucas is a lucky guy."

"I think I'm the lucky one but it doesn't hurt to have people telling me he's lucky too." I laugh. I'm laughing a lot but I can't help it. *I'm getting married today!*

"Are you ready?" Dad asks.

"Hell yes. Let's get this show on the road."

The three of us leave the room together and meet the girls at the back door. The door to the backyard of the main house on Drake Wines and leads me straight to the same arch that my Dad's, aunts and uncles all got married under.

I watch as the girls walk down the aisle and then the traditional wedding march plays, that's our cue to start our walk.

Dad takes my right arm gently in his and Jenni takes my left just as gently, in hers and the three of us make our way down the aisle to the love of my life.

When I spot Lucas standing at the arch with the celebrant, Giulia, I feel the tears well in my eyes. I feel like everything has come full circle. The man I love waiting to become my husband, in the same place that my Dads were married, the day before we arrived at Drake Wines to live here.

If Mum was here it would have been perfect.

Giulia asks who gives me away and Dad and Jenni say both of them and the crowd laughs and it's Dad who puts my hand in Lucas'. Then he sits next to Papa in the front row, who already has tears in his eyes and Jenni sits beside him, leaving a space in between them that I know would have been filled with by Mum.

Jenni thinks the clip in my hair means that my Mum is with me today but I know that she's with me because of the guardian angel charm I've got pinned inside my bra, right above my heart.

The ceremony starts and I realise life happened the way it was supposed to. I love my life and I loved growing up at Drake Wines.

Most of all, I loved spending the first nine years with my Mum and Jenni and the last twelve years with Dad and Papa and the rest of the crazy Drake bunch. This is where I was always supposed to be. It lead me to Lucas and for that I will forever be grateful.

As Giulia gets to the vows, I send up a silent thank you to Lori Stephenson, my beautiful Mum, who was taken too soon but is still very much loved and never forgotten.

DRAKE WINES SERIES IN READING ORDER:

VINEYARD Book .1. (M/F)
SANDY COVE A Novella 1.5 (M/F)
WINERY Book .2. (M/M)
LORI'S MEMORIES A Novella 2.5 (F)
BREWERY Book .3. (M/F)
SARA'S FOREVER A Novella 3.5 (F/M)

VINEYARD

Marriage. Babies. Live their happily ever after.

Makenna Drake and Brady Harris have been in love since they were sixteen years old, and they've had their future together planned out for almost as long.

Then Makenna's world is shattered when her parents are killed, and she's left to help her brothers keep the family business, Drake Wines, thriving.

Brady is determined to be her rock through the difficult times as she comes to terms with her loss, knowing that when their wedding goes ahead, they'll be one step closer to their happily ever after.

Until another tragic loss hits them, and they have to decide what their true definition of family is. They have to make the choice to redefine their dream of a family to achieve the happily ever after they long for.

VINEYARD is the first book in the Drake Wines Series. It's a steamy romance full of love and loss that will take you on a ride alongside the characters. Fall in love with Makenna and Brady today!

DRAKE WINES SERIES IN READING ORDER:

VINEYARD Book .1. (M/F)

SANDY COVE A Novella 1.5 (m/f)

WINERY Book .2. (M/M)

LORI'S MEMORIES A Novella 2.5 (F)

BREWERY Book .3. (M/F)

SARA'S FOREVER A Novella 3.5 (F/M)

SANDY COVE

Sun. Sand. Ocean. Paradise. Love?
Samantha Holt has worked alongside Bettie Bryant, owner and manager of the Sandy Cove Resort for years hoping to be given the chance to take over the reins when Bettie finally retires. She finally gets the chance but Bettie has one last surprise for her.

Tomas Jensen, the Adventure Specialist that Bettie hired without Samantha's knowledge.

Samantha is attracted to Tomas but she has her own set of rules about relationships with co-workers. She knows they don't work, so she's set a self-imposed banned on them. For herself anyway.

Samantha comes to realise that she needs to take a chance if she wants the sexiest, most infuriating man she's ever met. He's willing to give her that chance until a secret comes out that sends Tomas in a spin, demanding to know if her ex is the reason she won't give *him* a chance.

SANDY COVE is the first novella in the Drake Wines Novella Series and should be read after VINEYARD. It's a steamy romance full of love, sand and sunshine that will take you on a ride with characters. Fall in love with Samantha and Tomas, today!

WINERY

A creepy neighbour. A surprise from the past. A family of their own.

Logan Drake met Julian Bishop when he least expected it but that didn't stop him from grabbing the chance meeting with both hands. Gladly.

Jules supported Logan from the sidelines, through his parents death but when Logan's sister, Makenna, gets married and Julian can't actually *be* by Logan's side, that's when Jules decides enough is enough. After six years together in the shadows, he walks away.

As Logan tries to drink his way to oblivion every night, a family intervention brings him to a painful realisation. He lost the one person he needs more than anyone else. After telling Jules how he feels, he leaves their relationship in his hands. Luckily for Logan, love wins.

Except Ben, Jules' neighbour, isn't too happy that they've rekindled their relationship as things get creepy, Logan insists that Jules needs to move out to Drake Wines with him, where he can be safe. Then, just as life starts to settle down, someone from Logan's past returns, shocking them both. Will Logan and Julian's love be strong enough to survive the shock and changes involved with the surprise visit?

WINERY is the second book in the Drake Wines Series. It's a steamy M/M romance full of love and surprises that will take you on a ride with the characters. Fall in love with Logan and Jules today!

ALSO BY CHELLE PIMBLOTT:
BAREFOOT & DUMPED!

What would you do if your boyfriend dumped you at your parent's 30th wedding anniversary party?

LEXI

I know I should be more upset about my break up, but in reality there are only two reasons I'm annoyed. First and foremost, he did it before I could, and second, he did it at my freaking parent's party! Who does that? My ex douchebag that's who! Let's see how long I can drag out him picking up the tiny amount of crap he had at my place.

When my parent's insist that my sister and I leave their party to celebrate my break up, Lacey my best friend jumps on the chance and we're at our favourite bar drinking and dancing ourselves into oblivion, while sharing a table with a man that makes my skin sizzle. I have no time for someone new, even a one night stand, because I need to find me before I find another 'us'. I won't live to make someone else happy, or myself comfortable ever again.

GABE

Am I annoyed that Lexi hasn't called me yet? Yeah, I am, but I guess there could be a million reasons why she hasn't, and I'm just glad I was there to help her and her friends out. Happy to have made sure they were safe at the bar and then got home as well. I would hope someone would do it for my sister in similar circumstances.

When Lexi and I literally run into each other a week later, I can't believe my luck. It seems like the answer to all my prayers, until I realise she's freaked out because I know her name and she doesn't remember me, at all! As I watch her bolt, I know I have two choices, and I choose to walk away because I refuse to come across as any kind of creepy stalker. I've dealt with a crazy ex, and I won't do that to anyone. So, once again, I'm left without her number, and I decide to let it go. Let her go, but that's easier said than done.

When Lexi's ex plays a dangerous game, will Gabe be able to get to her in time to protect her?

AN EXCERPT from BAREFOOT & DUMPED!

L ate in the week, I'm checking messages on my phone as I walk to get a coffee from my favourite café. I'm barely paying attention, but I have to pause at the door to let a lady leave so that I can enter. Only when I walk in what I think is an open doorway, I find a hard wall of muscle instead. The impact of our bodies knocks my phone out of my hand and with the quickest reflexes I've ever seen, an arm reaches out and catches it before it can hit the ground and smash into pieces.

"Oh my god! Thank you so much for catching my phone and I'm so sorry about walking into you. I should have been watching where I was going, but I had a one track mind heading into buy the best lemon slice in the world."

My hand is still resting on the solid wall of his chest and I feel the rumble of his laughter work its way through his body before it finally reaches his vocal chords. Then it's the most amazing sound I've ever heard. I can't hear the traffic or anything else. "No worries. Things happen, there was no harm done at all."

There's something familiar about him, his face is registering as someone I know, but I know without a doubt, if I knew him from anywhere I'd remember him.

"Thank you." I say, my voice barely a husky whisper.

"You're welcome Lexi." He says, handing me my phone.

"Excuse me, but can I get past please? I need to get to work." Asks the guy behind Mr Hazel eyes, who has been patiently waiting for us to move out of the way.

"Yes, of course," I say as we both move out of the doorway to let the guy through. That's when it registers that this guy knew my name.

"I was hoping we could exchange phone numbers this time ..." I don't let the guy finish. What the hell is he talking about and how does he know my name?

"This time? How do you know my name?" He opens his mouth to speak, but I hold up my hand to stop him. "No actually, please don't say another word. I'm going to walk away now and forget this ever happened and hopefully we can live the rest of our lives happily knowing that I didn't let the creepy guy kill me." I don't let him say anything, I just take off in the opposite direction to where I'm supposed to be heading. I didn't do it on purpose, I just wanted to get away from the guy I don't know, but who seems to know me. I mean he knew my name and asked for my number. Who the hell does that?

I hear him call my name from behind me, but I don't look back, he's freaking me the hell out and I pick up my pace. I'm not quite jogging, because well heels, but I am definitely power walking at this stage, until I find myself ducking very quickly into an arts supplies store. I make a quick circle of the shelves so that I don't look like a crazy person to the lady behind the counter and then smile at her on my way out.

"Did you need some help to find what you were looking for?" She asks as I reach for the door and I panic.

"No. Thank you, I'm fine." I reply quickly, knowing I look and sound as sketchy as hell. No pun intended. Without another thought I shoot out the door and look up and down the street to see if the guy has gone. When I can't see him anywhere I head back the way I came, but I don't go into the bakery like I had intended before I ran into 'the guy', instead I walk, at quite an impressive pace, to work. I can't wait to meet up with Lacey for lunch later and tell her about my stalker. She's going to want to call in ASIO or the FBI or the CIA. I can't think of any other acronyms for any more government organisations. I'm pretty sure the American agencies don't have any authority in Australia, but that won't stop Lacey from trying.

BUILT TO LAST: Book .1. Built for Love Series

Kami's spent the last few years getting her book shop up and running. When she needs some renovations done, she asks for recommendations, and the overwhelming response is, Harvey Carpentry. So, when she sees the truck with the Harvey logo, she takes the chance, and asks for a quote. The guy who turns around is James freaking Harvey, and he still takes my breath away, just like he did in high school. Kami should have connected the Harvey name to James, but it didn't even occur to her.

James is working hard to distance himself from his father's reputation, but it hasn't been easy. Even as men employ him to work in their homes, they warn him to keep his hands on the job and off their wives. Then Kami Parker walks up to his truck asking for a quote and James can't believe his luck. Now that they're adults maybe she can see that he's a guy worth spending time with. Maybe even a lifetime?

AN EXCERPT from BUILT TO LAST

I close my eyes because, after the tension and electricity that was just zapping around us not 5 minutes ago, everything I say seems to have a sexual undertone to it. I'm not even trying, for the first time in a long time, but it sure does seem to be coming out that way. I clear my throat and go to speak again but Kami beats me to it.

"Did you *make* an apple pie ... for me?" She asks. Here I was thinking that she'd gotten past my cooking skills, apparently not.

"Yes Kami, I made an apple pie, from scratch, for dessert. For you, well yeah cause you're here but I also felt like eating an apple pie, so I made one."

"From scratch?" I slowly nod my head in answer to her question because I can't be bothered voicing the same answer, again. "Wow! Umm yes, please, can I have some cream on top?"

I groan at the double meaning and dish us both up a slice of pie with cream on top. I can't even look at her, the thoughts that are rolling around my head, if I look at her I'm sure she'll be able to read my mind and go running out my door. Then I'll have lost the only chance I have with this beautiful woman. I've waited so long to have this chance, an opportunity to prove to her that I'm not as bad as everyone thinks, I can't get ahead of myself. It may have been a mistake to cook dinner for her and bring her out to my home, but even if it is, I wouldn't change it for anything. Well, except maybe an overnight stay with her, which included me getting to do all the things I want to with her.

Her groan snaps me out of my head and makes my cock instantly hard. When I look across the table at her, she's got her eyes closed, and she's licking her lips. My spoon is hovering somewhere between my bowl and my mouth, while I watch Kami take another mouthful of my apple pie to her mouth, open wide and moan again as she closes her mouth around the spoon. Fuck me, she's killing me, but what a way to die.

Her eyes open as she tells me, "Holy heck James, this is delicious. I swear it's the best thing I've had in my mouth in, forever." Then she realises what she's said as my jaw drops to the table and the cream starts to drip off my spoon. I should have changed out of my jeans, there isn't enough fucking room in them to eat dinner with this woman. "I, ummm, didn't mean that the way it came out. It's ... you're a really good cook James."

"Thank you Kami, coming from you, that means a lot." I say.

"Why? You don't even know if I can cook, I could be really bad for all you know, I mean I *do* go to the café every day for lunch." She laughs, and it's become my favourite sound in the last couple of days. "Maybe next time, you can come to my house and I'll cook for you?" Her whole body freezes as she realises what she's just said, and her spoon clangs back into her bowl.

"That's a deal Kami. Next time it's at your place and you're cooking for me." Without another word about it, I pick up my bowl and hers and take them to the sink. "Let's look at the plans I drew up for the renovations shall we?" It seems like it might be a safer subject right now and it should, with any luck, help my hard on become less hard!

BUILT FOR TROUBLE: Book .2. Built for Love Series

Can Katy forgive Joe's past behaviour to move towards a future together? Does love win over friendship?

Joe made Katy's best friend's life hell when they were at High School, but even then, there was still something that always drew her to him. When they start seeing each other at a local café where they both go for lunch, and share a table to, 'save space', they get to know each other as adults, and they like what they see.

When Joe asks Katy out for dinner, a date is set. One that neither of them ever saw coming. Especially given their past, but sometimes things happen for a reason. The draw to one another is electric and unrelenting .... unforgiving.

When Joe explains his reason for giving her best friend so much grief, something even more shocking is revealed in the process.

Can their relationships survive all the pain and grief that these revelations cause? Will love win in the end? The love between a man and a woman. The love between friends?

AN EXCERPT from BUILT FOR TROUBLE

"Does this dress of yours have a zip or buttons or can I just pull it off your body honey'?" I growl in her ear, as my hands wander all over her back trying to find how I can get her out of the damned thing.

"Mmmm." Is all I get out of her as she continues teasing my nipples and kissing along my jawline.

Kissing up her neck I ask in a husky whisper in her ear," Katy, tell me how to get this thing off or I'm just going to rip it off you."

"Mmmm," she moans again, then she seems to shake her head for a second and says, "Zip. At. The. Side." She hisses out between breaths and kisses.

I don't know who designed this damned thing, but it wasn't with an idea of getting anyone out of it in a fucking hurry that's for sure. My hands run up and down her sides, trying to find the zipper so that I can put my hands , my mouth and whatever else I can get on this woman. The dress needs to go, now.

"Katy," I groan against her neck, "Babe, I need to put you down for a second."

"Mmmm." Is her only response. She looks delectable, with her head leaning back against the door, making her neck stretch out and all I want to do is lick it and nibble on it.

Instead, I let her leg fall off my hip and place her foot on the floor, my hand gripping her hip. My other hand pulls down the zipper of her dress letting it fall to her waist. I let out what can only be described as an animalistic growl, a vocal declaration of the desire that's coursing through my body.

"Joe." Katy's voice is soft, husky and full of her own desire.

"Yes, Katy?" I reply. "What do you need babe?"

"You, I need you, Joe. God, I need you everywhere Joe."

"Everywhere? How do I get everywhere baby?"

"I don't know, I just know what I need." Her hands are running through my hair, over my shoulders, grasping my neck and running her nails up and down my back. It's like she can't get enough of me and I sure as fuck know I can't get enough of her.

"I know baby, I feel the same way. I'm trying to get us there but this dress.."

SNEAKY: Book .1. Sneaky Love Series

When love sneaks up on you, do you run with it or run away?

Ally is a quirky baker who dreams of running her own bakery. She's sworn off men after her last boyfriend cheated on her multiple times. She's more than happy to concentrate on going into partnership with her best friend Georgie, to fulfil both of their dreams. The only problem is, the contractor Georgie hired is hard to handle!

Alex is bowled over by the baker that smells like the sugar and chocolate she plans on cooking with once he gets her kitchen built for her. She might be as tiny as a pixie but she's got walls he wants to break down, even after Georgie warns him off her best friend, he can't resist her.

Will they fight their feelings and each other or will they give in the building feelings between them?

AN EXCERPT from SNEAKY

S hit, shit, shit, shit..
I can't believe we just had sex in my brand new kitchen. A kitchen I'll be cooking food for the public in, *very* soon. Ohhhh my god. This is definitely not a food safe activity.

"I can't believe we just did that Alex." I squeal as I untangle myself from the mountain of a man who just gave me 2 orgasms in like maybe 10 minutes, if that.

"I know Pixie, that was AMAZING." He replies but I'm pushing against his chest, trying to get him to move away from me. We have to get this mess and ourselves cleaned up.

"No Alex." I say, then I see the look on his face and continue, "I mean yes it *was amazing,* but this is a commercial kitchen. It needs to be food grade, you know, clean enough to cook food in to sell to the paying customer. I have to get everything cleaned up, and properly. What if someone walks in here and sees all of this ...." I gesture around the room with my arms open wide. That's when I realise that I'm bare-arsed naked, and standing in the middle of my kitchen, my *commercial* kitchen in the new bakery that we're about to open to the public.

"We have to get dressed. I can't believe .... I can't believe I just did that."

"Ally. Ally calm down. No-one is going to walk in here ....."

"You did. You just waltzed on in, and I didn't even realise you were there until it was too late. Maybe someone has already seen us, and they're just waiting for us to get our shit together so they can ...."

"So they can what Ally? Huh?" He asks as he pulls on his jeans. "I think you're forgetting that I had a *key, Ally*. I'm going to *assume* there are only 3 people who have one, unless you, and Georgie hand them out like lollies that is. "

"Of course we don't just hand the keys out to anyone who asks. I didn't even know *you* had a key for fucksake, and trust me I'll be asking my business partner all about that one." I say. I can't believe that Georgie gave out a key to our business, and didn't even bother telling me.

"Georgie gave me a key so that neither of you two ladies had to be here at the arse crack of dawn to let myself or my crew in to start work every day. At the time, we thought it was a brilliant idea. Sorry that me having a key has inconvenienced you tonight *Ally*, I'll get out of your hair just as soon as I've helped you clean up 'our mess', ok?"

I look up at Alex after getting myself put back together, only to find him looking at me with anger. What did I do? He's angry because I'm annoyed that Georgie didn't tell me she'd given him a key? I grab the nearby broom to start sweeping up the flour that's managed to spread everywhere, and say to him, "It's not an inconvenience Alex, it's just that I would have appreciated knowing that there was another key out there. Like tonight for instance. I didn't worry about the noises because I knew I'd locked everything up, and I thought only 2 people had keys. I didn't know you were able to get in here without my knowledge."

"Well Ally, I'm very sorry that I interrupted you, and came in the bakery without your knowledge. I guess I should be leaving now and let you get back to it."

"What? So now you're not even going to help me clean up this mess? Awesome. Just great. Thanks a heap Alex." I don't know why he's so angry, especially after we just had the best sex of my life. Oh, hang on does he think ....

SNEAKING AROUND: Book .2. Sneaky Love Series

C an she get him to get out of his head long to admit his feelings or will she be the little sister he doesn't have?

For Mia, Dan has always been a part of her life, he's her brother Alex's best friend and he's been family forever. She's also had a crush on him for as long as she can remember and it only got worse the older they got.

Dan has fought his attraction to his best friend and business partners sister for so long now it feels like a second skin. Alex knows him better than anyone but if he knew what he was thinking when he looked at Mia, there's no way he'd still be my friend. that's why I have to keep my distance.

When they finally give in to desire, will Alex be able to accept them being together or will their happiness be short lived?

AN EXCERPT from SNEAKING AROUND

I shouldn't touch her. I should let her leave, but I don't. I can't. I grab her flailing hand, and pull her to me, our chests meeting with a dull thud. I hold her hand over my rapidly beating heart. I know I shouldn't, but I do it anyway. I need the touch. My other hand reaches up behind her neck, and slowly, I bend her head backwards, so that I can reach her lips. Our lips aren't touching, but they're only a breath away, I could easily reach out my lips and kiss her. My eyes haven't left hers, and I'm watching every reaction she has to me. She hasn't pulled away, that's always a good sign.

"If you tell me to stop Mia, I will, and we can forget anything happened. But, if you don't tell me to stop now, I don't think I'll be able to." She takes in a deep breath, never once looking away from my eyes. "Answer me now Mia, I'll only ask this once. *Do you want me to kiss you, sweet cheeks?*"

Goddamnit, if she says no, I'm fucked!

She takes a deep breath, holds it for a few seconds. I start to let her go, I've completely screwed this up, and I can't take it back. She's my best friend's sister, and I have to see her way too often to have let it get this far.

Before I can move away from her, she drops her bag, and grabs the hand holding hers onto my chest. Her voice is husky and sure, "Dan Robson, if you don't kiss me now, I'm going to punch you so fucking hard ....."

That's all the permission I need! Within a split second, my lips are on hers. Gently for just a minute, and then she gasps as I pull her hips to mine. I know she can feel my hard cock rubbing against her stomach. I put my knee between her legs and rub against her. She's warm, and wet, I can feel her through my jeans. She groans, and I slide my tongue in her mouth, tangling it with hers. I can't get enough.

GOD! Why did I wait so fucking long? She's like heaven! I've never felt this rush or need with anyone else!

NO MORE SNEAKING AROUND: Book .3. Sneaky Love Series

Happily Ever After Guaranteed!

ALLY & ALEX

They're making the most of every business opportunity they can. Ally is tired on top of her tired and Alex is worried about her pushing herself too far.

Alex's construction business is going so well that he and Dan had to employ another crew. He's also learned to live with his best friend and his sister living together but is Dan doesn't look after Mia, then there will be hell to pay.

MIA & DAN

They're happily living together with Alex's blessing with an underlying promise to pull Dan into line if he messes up.

Alex's threat doesn't worry Dan because he knows a secret that's going to blow Alex's mind.

Dan is also working hard to bring in more clients for his carpentry business.

MAX & JORDAN - A BONUS STORY

Mia's best friend Max, is looking for love but he's been hurt before, burned by trusting the wrong people with his heart.

With a history filled with pain because of those who were supposed to love and protect him, but didn't, he has a choice to make. Can he trust himself and Jordan so that he can have the happily ever after that he deserves?

AN EXCERPT from NO MORE SNEAKING AROUND

"I think we're both lucky to have to finally found each other, Sweetcheeks. I was very happy to just be married to you but you giving me our children, *that's* something else my love." I bend over and kiss her forehead.

I thought in that moment that I couldn't be happier but I was wrong. SO wrong! The day the twins were born was, what can I say, it was incredible! I felt like I might cop a broken hand but it was about *more* than my agony because Mia pushed not one, but *two* not so tiny humans out of her body! My bruised hand, well that just doesn't count for a fucking second! At least that's what the midwife tells me anyway and I have to say, I'm inclined to agree with her and not *just* because she could make my death look like an accident but because she's also right!

Twins! Born naturally and absolutely perfect and I'm more in love with them and their mother than I ever thought possible. I thought I was protective of little Jessica, but you've got no idea what I'm like with these two precious bundles Mia gave me! I even gave Alex a lecture on how he wasn't holding one of my babies correctly! The look he gave me *could* have thawed Antarctica! Then he burst out into a belly laugh and once he caught his breath, he said, "Now Dan, I know where you're coming from and it means you're going to be the best father I could ever hope for but Dickwad, I've held a baby before!"

I can't help the chuckle that escapes me as I remember that exchange! It doesn't escape me at all that I'm sitting here, on Alex's deck with our wives and children and how domesticated we all look!

Alex is at the BBQ, cooking up lunch. We have lunch now, not dinner, that way the kids can be in bed and asleep early, hopefully!

Ally is reclining on a lounger, her hands resting on her growing belly, yup they're expecting baby number 2, while Jessie crawls around her chair and trying to pull herself up on her feet!

Then I look over to the chair next to Allycat, and there's my wife sitting and feeding our son, Jack. He's a hungry little devil, I just hope he leaves a little something for his sister. After I've changed her nappy and clothes, it will be her turn for a feed. Then, hopefully, if we've timed it right, the twins will sleep so that we can have an uninterrupted meal for once. Just once!

Ohhh Yeah, I forgot to mention that part, didn't I? The twins, we got one of each! Molly Grace Robson and Jack Ryder Robson. We didn't plan on starting with double the trouble but here we are! I don't think we'll be in any hurry to add to the brood, the twins are more than enough for now.

As I look out and take everything in, I can't help the huge smile that's plastered on my face. I got the girl and we got a family. I never thought this is where I would end up, but I wouldn't have it any other way.

"What are you looking all goofy about Dickwad? The smell of dirty nappies finally gotten to your brain man?"

"Nah Dipshit, just thinking about lucky we are man."

"Guys, language! Jessie will be copying everything you say soon and I don't want her calling anyone Dipshit or Dickwad, thank you very much!"

"Sorry Ally." We say at the same time and then burst out laughing. I can't imagine that angel repeating those words but I guess you never can tell!

Don't miss out!

Visit the website below and you can sign up to receive emails whenever Chelle pimblott publishes a new book. There's no charge and no obligation.

https://books2read.com/r/B-A-FGVL-GUQPB

BOOKS 2 READ

Connecting independent readers to independent writers.

www.ingramcontent.com/pod-product-compliance
Lightning Source LLC
Chambersburg PA
CBHW070636120726
47909CB00004B/1464